Out of
Their Shadows

Out of Their Shadows

RANJANA KAMO

PARTRIDGE
A Penguin Random House Company

To order additional copies of this book, contact
Partridge India
000 800 10062 62
orders.india@partridgepublishing.com

www.partridgepublishing.com/india

Acknowledgements

———◆※◆———

I would like to thank my mother Mrs. Raj Kamo who has stood by me through my life. She encouraged me as I spent long hours in penning down this book. She also took some time out of her schedule to help in proof reading the final draft of my book.

I would like to thank my father Mr. Ramesh Chander Kamo for showering his blessings from heaven.

I would also like to thank my brother Ramnik and sister-in-law Garima for always being so supportive.

I am thankful for the weekends that provided me the opportunity to tap my fingers on the keyboard of my laptop and manage writing this book.

Above all it is God's will as nothing is possible without his support. I would like to thank Him for His blessings and divine light that designed my life and helped me write this book.

Preface

I have often seen people give up easily and many a times just at the brink of success. There are social pressures to take up jobs and careers suited to your socio-economic or family status which could be just in contrast to your aptitude and interest. This leads to frustration which keeps building within the individual and is bound to be destructive over time. I have also observed many a times that some individuals are unaware of the great talents hidden in their personalities which seem to take a backseat in the daily humdrum of life's tensions and worries. Life can definitely be at its best when we get an opportunity to build on our talents and find success and this does not seem to happen too often. There is another element to being successful which is the willingness to mentor talents and help others in achieving their goals which brings real happiness in its wake.

"Out Of Their Shadows" touches upon these subjects and builds around the life of two individuals trying to discover the purpose and aim of their existence. The story takes them through the undulating path of their life together through failures, successes, love and much more to redesign their destiny.

All the characters and places as well as the incidents described in the book are imaginary and any resemblance to someone/ someplace/ something could only be a mere coincidence.

This book is a product of five weeks of relentless work. There is an element of myself in every character that I create and readers should be able to relate to them with ease as their issues and struggles are realistic.

With love to Neel, Ruhi and Nina....

Chapter 1

We are the true reflections of the colours of our souls and the stark irony is that it takes us a lifetime to explore and understand these colours from the collage of infinite images built over time. There is a grand spectrum of hues spanning our personalities but we tend to overlook the brightest ones in our feeble attempts to manage with the faintest colours to juggle through our lives with painstaking difficulties. There is no denying that there is an element of poetry in these phrases and so is the design of our lives that has poetry flowing through it with a plethora of emotions with each shade and each colour that defines every life.

Our lives are designed perfectly but we complicate them with our insecurities and dwindling confidence that narrows our perspective about the design of our lives restricting ourselves to a limited area while there is ample vacant space available to create and recreate designs to suit our priorities. There are some who are fortunate to discover the brightness of their soul's rainbow whereas many do not even realize that it exists within them.

Life throws open more challenges than one can manage at all times creating ripples of distraught with failed attempts dominating the field of our life. Each individual has a capacity to take on challenges and the colours of the soul determine the level of endurance but it is the awareness of that level which marks the winning streaks on the expeditious track of life. The real challenge lies in discovering this level or the potential that truly defines a person which could turn into a lifelong project for many as they do not find it throughout their lives while there are some who are able to explore their best potentials by accident and a small percentage find a mentor in people around them to guide them towards this exploration.

The key to success lies in the discovery of the potential that truly defines a person, a strength that gives a soul a purpose, a real meaning to its very existence in the world and the ability to nurture that potential to sow the seeds that lead to great achievements on the undulating cobbled path of life. The design of life is destined as some might say and some carve it out as per their desire by delving into their soul to extract its strongest colours and explore the excellence of their purpose in this world where life and it's grandeur are superbly aligned in a perfect angle to outshine it's very design.

Chapter 2

Nita is one such person who is unaware of the colours that line her soul as she walks through the world like a lost fledgling with the sole purpose in life to find its nest. Nita, the timid girl, who tries to meander through her life with a wavering confidence on an aimless path where road maps are not clearly drawn and road signs are obscure to misplace her true identity like an abandoned ship that has drifted far away from land. A five and a half feet tall, fair and petite girl who loves to confide in her toys who are her best friends, a nervous soul who avoids the world as much as she possibly can, a gentle being who finds peace within herself and is unaware of the power that exists within her, an angel without her wings looking at the skies with a hope to flap her imaginary wings into a flight to the unknown. Little does Nita know that her attempts to create an imaginary world to face the real one are futile but she has an uncontrollable urge to define a world of her own that can shelter her from the cold and bitterness of the outside world which appears to be a harsh bed of thorns to her as experiences of her life have revealed to her in her past. The boundaries of her imaginary world create a fence for her that contains her happiness within the borders of her own world, a world that knows no pain, no worries and no sorrow.

Nita first opened her eyes in a hospital in Saloni, a beautiful modern city on the foothills of the magnanimous range of the tall mountains called Aseem Mountains which stand like mammoth giants lining the sky of Saloni and narrating the tales of its ancient history that has richness in its great culture and diversity in its population that is primarily from settlers from across the nation. Saloni is known for its mystic gardens that line every boundary and street of the city embellishing its life with ornamental hues from the colours of the wondrous varieties of flowers that adorn them. She

15

has been brought up in the cradle of the beautiful valley of Saloni where she lives with her parents in a plush bungalow which is abundantly packed with wealth and defines richness in its enormously radiant blueprints of grandeur. She has studied in the most reputed school and college of Saloni before she did her post-graduation from the University of Saloni, a name to reckon with in the educational world. Her credentials are commendable and her family very supportive, loving and caring; her parents run their own flourishing businesses and have created a lifestyle where dearth is fortunately unknown and life is as comfortable as comfort can be and is overflowing with wealth and where prosperity knows no bounds. Nita does not know the meaning of the word 'want' but she knows that there is 'something' she does not have. She senses it when she walks up to talk to someone but fumbles in her attempt to speak, or when she hides within herself at a party or a mall to become invisible from the people surrounding her, or when her feet start trembling when she is asked to participate in a debate or make a presentation to a group of people making her shy away from public meetings. She loves to spend all her time with her best friend Mini in the cozy shell of her well decorated room of her extravagantly designed home which has been named Ashiana by her mother. Nita knows there is 'something' that is missing which makes her nervous and this 'something' is the confidence that her friend Mini can boast of possessing in large doses as the world greets her with great respect and looks up to her as she seems to rule the world.

Mini is the smartest person that Nita has ever known and she is awed by Mini's superiorly confident persona that helps her face the world with the magical ease unknown to Nita. The world loves to hear Mini and bows to her when she enters any meeting, party or an office and unrolls a red carpet for her to step on and walk through the cavalry around her royal power. Nita takes pride in walking with Mini as Mini is the 'superior being' who is capable of achieving the impossible with no effort involved. Mini has an infectious smile that captivates everyone who happens to be around her, charming the world and walking through every difficulty with poise and elegance as a star that owns and rules the world. Nita just cannot stop admiring her and wishes to be as graceful as Mini and imbibe her confidence in every stance of her life. She loves to walk with Mini and see the adulation she gets from the world as she wishes to glide through her life with the same supreme enigmatic charisma that defines Mini, the mini goddess.

It is a beautiful morning that sees Nita waking up to the music of the mountains which seem to be humming with the breeze blowing through the trees in the valley and waking the sleepy flowers with a touch of its soft feathers that gently fondle their petals to awaken their blooms to greet the morning with their sweet smiles.

Nita calls out to Mini. "Mini, please wake up. Wakey, wakey!! It is time to get up and go for the job interview." Mini smiles and opens her eyes as the morning greets her long black tresses with its golden yellow brightness as the orange sun smiles through its shining rays from the clear blue skies and birds chirp their morning song merrily. The light from the window panes is trickling in with a hope that this day would introduce Nita to a confident spirit that she can hold onto and walk through the job interview she has been called for. Mini and Nita get ready for the day with hopes of marking the day as a successful one in the calendar of their life. Nita wants to look her best and takes Mini's help in choosing her dress and Mini's choice is always the best so Nita gets to wear her best outfit this morning. Nita's mother Kaya Sain calls her from the foot of the staircase leading to Nita's room asking her to join her at the breakfast table and this makes Nita nervous. Kaya manages a business house set up by Shan Sain, her loving and extremely caring husband whose only aim in life is to see his wife and daughter happy by giving them every comfort possible and pamper their life extravagantly with riches and luxuries. Kaya markets the top brands in cosmetics while Shan owns several car dealerships and together they make billions in an year which give them the opulent lifestyle that can make anyone envious of their prosperity. Kaya and Shan dote on their daughter and only child Nita who is literally the apple of their eyes with pink cheeks and a fair delicate skin and dark brown eyes that are frequently concealed by her pitch black hair that keep falling on her face with the sweet caress of the gentle breeze. They want to set up a business for Nita but are let down by her constant refusal which leaves them worried and disappointed as they worry for her future which is covered in haze at present as Nita has not tried to step out of her world till now. Nita is unable to accept the tempting proposal as she fears making mistakes and lacks confidence to face people making her avoid talking to her parents and attempting to quietly sneak into her room every time she sees them around. The very thought of managing the business leaves her nervous and she makes an excuse each time Kaya or Shan try to speak to her about their plans for her business. They want to set up a travel agency for her but she trembles at the thought of managing clients and staff and being surrounded by people who would judge her abilities and mock her follies and probably hurt her with their snide remarks on her shortcomings. Nita is aware of her drawbacks and wants to overcome her fears and that makes her look for a job that will help her build her confidence before she can independently launch her own business.

"Nita, please finish your breakfast before you leave. And I need to speak to you before you plan to disappear for the day," Kaya calls out to Nita from the dining hall. Nita is shaken up from her comfort zone as the question about the business haunts her and all her attempts to avoid it are unfortunately turning futile. She walks out from her bedroom with reluctance and a hope that her mother will not ask her the same question again. She has a nervous look on her face as she responds feebly to her mother with terror spelt boldly in her tense dark brown eyes, "Okay, Mom." Nita's looks imply that she would be soon put on the altar and sacrificed to fulfill her mother's wishes and thrown into the cruel arms of the business they are setting up for her. Kaya notices Nita's nervousness as she approaches the dining hall with her baby steps and tries to calm her down, "Nita, I am not going to eat you up. You know your Mom loves you. Dad and I are trying our best to have you settled in a business so that you can have a comfortable life and never face the need to depend on anyone for anything. You should feel fortunate to have this opportunity which many would give anything to have." Nita nods her head but is still very nervous fearing that she is incapable of handling such a big responsibility. "What if?" is the big question that blocks her view of life! "What if I fail? What if I am unable to manage the business? What if I am not able to handle people? What if I run into losses? What if I am questioned? What if I do not have all the answers? What if I get laughed at or ridiculed? What if ….," there is a never ending list of questions that clouds her mind and vision adding to the infinite confusions of her nervous disposition leaving her totally unsettled at the wide crossroads of her life. Shan looks at Kaya and then at Nita and decides not to interfere in the mother daughter conversation but cannot help adding his comments as he looks at them with concern through his gold rimmed spectacles that circle his black eyes. "Nita, your mom is right. You need to take this up soon, the sooner the better. Go for it daughter!" Nita nods again and looks at her parents and then turns to Mini. "Mini, what should I do? What do you think is right? Are you okay with this idea? I am too nervous at the very thought of managing it. Do you think I can manage it?" Mini nods in agreement and asks her to go ahead, a nod that is always the final judgement for Nita who blindly believes in her discretion. "Nita, where are you lost and whom are you talking to?" asks Kaya as she frowns at her daughter. Nita looks at Mini and then at her Mom and back at Mini again. "She pretends that she does not see you Mini but I know Mom knows you are here with me," Nita whispers to Mini. "Can I go for this last job interview Mom and then we can discuss about the business in the evening," Nita says in her faltering voice as she looks at Kaya, Shan and Mini in succession in a hope to get support from at least one of them but does not see much help coming. "What interview? Why do you want to go for any interview? You need to take up this business soon. You don't need to look for a job when you are eventually going to manage the travel agency," Kaya tells Nita. "One last time, Mom, please, just this one, please, one last time," pleads Nita. Kaya nods her head and tells her firmly, "Ok, this is the last time you are going for a job interview. We will finalize the details for your business today evening itself. Try to be back soon," Kaya tells Nita assertively. Nita thanks Kaya and she and Mini step out of their home, Ashiana.

Their home is called Ashiana, a huge villa in the posh Dilnar neighbourhood, a mile from the road that leads to Aseem Mountains. A huge white iron gate welcomes you to Ashiana with rose bushes lining the driveway to the porch. A villa with six bedrooms and luxury sprawled in the expensive furniture and décor of every room spread over the two floors of the house that has the warmth of love that bonds the family together. Nita is happy to be away from the pressing question about the travel business and smiles at Mini. "Mini, we need to be very confident for the interview today. Just wish I can get this job. There is this funny feeling in my stomach Mini. Do you think I will get this job? Don't know what questions will be put across to us? I am very scared of facing the interviewer. What if I do not know the answers Mini? I don't want to look like an idiot at the interview. Wish I could get the job without the interview. Do you think I will make it through the interview today?" Nita asks Mini for an affirmation and encouragement to face the interview board with confidence. Mini smiles at her and encourages her, "Of course Nita, you will make it. Just keep calm and confident." Nita tries to keep her calm but her nervousness reappears and she freezes. She stops as she is walking towards her car. It is a moment which has her petrified at the thought of being questioned and interviewed with strange eyes peering at her and passing judgement about her. Her eyes are moist as she recalls her bitter experience from the last interview which made her feel like a loser and a nobody in this world of achievers. Her face is lined with pain as the echo of the insulting remarks from Simon pierce through her heart. She had met Simon last week for a job at his office. Her inability to answer his questions had instigated him to ridicule her. His remarks had been very sharp and had left deep wounds across her heart and soul. She was made to look like an inferior being incapable of achieving anything in her life discouraging the little confidence that she had managed to build to help her talk to Simon. Her thoughts then move to another interview last month where the lady had a smirk on her face as she spoke to her adding to her nervousness. She had asked Nita some questions and gaped at her with disinterest when Nita could not manage to speak up. She had very blatantly and bluntly told her, "How will you work here? You cannot even speak one single sentence without faltering and fumbling. Do you think you can work here at all? How will you face anyone and get things done when you are so nervous and unsure about yourself. I am surprised at how you must be surviving in this world. I am sorry but I cannot offer you any position in my office." Nita recalls all the bitter experiences that she can from her past job interviews and looks nervously at Mini with her eyes telling her that she cannot go for this interview. She explains her apprehensions and the fear of facing people and being laughed at to Mini who listens to her intently and thinks through the problem at hand. Mini is always a good companion and a good listener who manages to calm Nita under all adverse situations as she understands her too well. Nita feels fortunate to have Mini by her side whose advice and motivation keep Nita moving ahead in life. She gives Nita the limbs and courage to forge ahead in spite of her nervousness, she makes her believe in herself and constantly motivates her to inspire her to outdo herself. Mini tells her to go for the interview and they ask their driver Manoj to drive them to Shagun Street, a commercial area in the heart of Saloni housing many offices, institutes and shopping complexes.

Kaya looks at Shan and shakes her head in her disappointment. "I worry for Nita, she makes me tense, ………don't know what she will do in her life? I am so nervous thinking about her lack of confidence in herself, wonder how I can help her out,…..feel so helpless, so torn, I really want to see her be on her own but she is locked within herself and the only place that interests her is her room,…..how do I help her come out of her cocoon and bloom into a beautiful flower in the world of reality, she cannot spend her life hiding from the real world?" Kaya confides her fears in Shan who makes an effort to show his indifference as he does not want to add to his wife's growing worries. He shares her fears about Nita but finds it inappropriate to talk about them with her at this delicate moment when she is emotionally distraught so he decides to cheer her up with some soothing and uplifting words. "She will be fine as she faces life, things will improve, have faith in her and in God, she is our child, she will soon take charge of her life," Shan tries to pacify Kaya with his caring words though Kaya's worry has sparked tension in his mind too, the tension of the fear of seeing his daughter losing out in the race of life and the possible pain from losing. Kaya's moist eyes have untold stories in them, tales of her love for her daughter, her worries for her life, the growing insecurity about what future holds in store for her, the fear of unfolding of life's obstacles that may bar her from moving ahead in life, masking her success from her, preventing her from her achievements and the unnerving sensation of the pain of failures that may mar her happiness and make her revert to a life of recluse. Shan looks out of the window and says a prayer in his mind, a prayer for their daughter's success in life, a prayer that holds the fears of caring parents for their daughter whom they love more than anything else in this world, a prayer to make the world turn in their daughter's favour to make her life change for the better and to instill great confidence in her to face life and its challenges. Kaya sits there in deep thought with the chimes on the terrace striking their arms to tune into a beautiful song, a premonition that Shan's prayers have been heard and there is a favourable verdict on its way to relieve Kaya of her worries and bring cheer in their life. The chiming is like a soft instrumental music that is bringing positive vibes with its notes to soothe the tense atmosphere that has built up in Ashiana from the worries that haunt Kaya and Shan. The arms of the chime entwine and loosen up in successive sequence with the cool breeze creating a heavenly music for the soul alleviating Kaya and Shan's worries a little.

Nita does not want to get off the car but gathers some courage to do so and walks into the office of the advertisement firm where she has applied for the job of a computer operator, a job that will help her stay behind a desk, far away from the questioning and judging eyes of people where she can work in solitude. The office is huge making her feel lost again with the multitude of people moving around swiftly and the constant sound of their shoes clicking as they walk through the corridor of the office with Nita's heartbeat increasing with her fear and her limbs trembling. The voice of the people mingles with the tapping of the keyboards and she can even hear their echoes through the glass walls that separate the cabins. "This is like a gas chamber, I will suffocate to death here, I don't want to work here, I am not at all comfortable here, let us leave Mini, I do not wish to speak to anyone here," Nita blurts out in her anguish to Mini. Mini holds her hand and tells her to keep calm and wait for the firm's owner to call her for the interview. Nita finds it impossible to wait in this gas chamber filled with monsters that might rip her apart any minute now making her fidget and lean on a pillar for support. Nita jumps up as she hears someone call out her name, the shrillness of the voice leaves her startled. She turns around to see a lady waiting for her and pushes herself to take a few steps in her direction while her heart is thumping and her legs are giving away as her heart beat is increasing at an unnerving speed. She hears her heart beat loudly and then she hears garbled voices at a distance and the strange ringtone of somebody's mobile in the background that is slowly turning into a message for her, "Nita, you are not needed here, you need to leave now, there is no place for a weakling like you here, you have to leave now." She freezes again as she is trying to walk up to the lady with the message through the ringtone repeating itself as a warning to her, her hand moves around to grope Mini's, her only support at that moment, whom she holds by her hand and grips her firmly and looks around with her terrified eyes before she screams, "Run, Mini, run," and she runs out of the office pulling Mini out with her as she thinks of herself as a warrior successfully making an escape from a dungeon. She runs out in a mad rush and stops near her car panting and huffing and of course, totally breathless but relieved to be out of the clutches of the vampires that were waiting to devour her inside the gas chamber. She looks at Mini and says, "We are safe now. That place was a terrifying torture house. I could not have survived there even for five minutes. I cannot work like this, just cannot. Let us go home. I would rather die in my travel agency than die in this gas chamber of glass."

Mini looks at Nita in disbelief, "You just had to go for the interview and answer a few questions, that's all and you ruined it." Mini looks at Nita with her anguish turning into anger which makes Nita realize her mistake. "Did I? Oh Mini, I am so sorry, what do we do now?" Nita regrets her action and feels sorry for disappointing Mini. Mini shakes her head in utter disappointment and looks around the street which is very busy and there are buildings lining both sides of the street with multiple options to choose from. "Another ten minutes and you could have made it Nita, you just ruined it, you could have managed it with ease and patience but you gave up the race even before crossing the start line," Mini grumbles in her disgusted voice making Nita feel sorry for her rather silly behaviour and a feeling of guilt overpowers her making her feel apologetic for her decision of running away from the office. Life does not always give you too many choices but it does respect those who make a choice and give it their best to carve a niche for themselves. Life has been giving Nita a number of choices but she closes the gates even before opening them as there is just one gate that she finds comfort in walking through, the gate of her room, her shell, that does not question her or assess her or judge or evaluate her personality but gives her a cozy and warm corner to be at ease and just be herself!

Mini looks around as she does not want to go home defeated, her mind in deep thought and her eyes wandering through the signboards on the road for a ray of hope that can help them sway a victory flag in the air. It takes her some time to look around the street to find the dart that could hit the bull's-eye with ease and help them in their mission that they have set out on. She thinks for a while and comes up with a grand idea which makes Nita feel a little better. "Why don't we join personality development classes at the Arts School? Just look across the street, that red building behind the huge lawns that you can see through the iron gate is the Arts School," Mini puts forth her suggestion as she points to the building with a huge board that looks inviting as it has the name "Arts School" written on it in a bold and beautiful font with a picture of a boy and girl holding a flag on the side. Nita gives it a serious thought as she remembers her mother's words that motivate her to join the classes before she is dragged into the business her parents are setting up for her. "Yes, you are right. In fact, you are always right Mini. Let us do it." Nita feels at ease and they leave for the Arts School on Shagun Street. Yes, Mini is always right and so is Nita. An alter ego has the strange and significant characteristic of being your body double! Knowing your shortcoming is a step towards success and accepting it is the next step towards excellence! Nita knows her drawback and today she has accepted it and is willing to make an effort to overcome her shortcoming as she walks towards the red building holding Mini's hand. Life is designing her destiny as she confronts the gate of the Arts School which looks like a gateway to a different world, a gate to all solutions, a gateway to successful aspirations, the doorway to a bright future, her future. Nita stands in front of the black gate and says her prayers as she peeps through the grills to see the expanse of the garden in front of the building. Nita is a little hesitant to walk into the Arts School as the fear of meeting teachers and new people grips her again making her immobile. The enormous gates of the school leave her intrigued and nervous at the same time. She is apprehensive of what lies ahead beyond the huge gates of the Arts School. This is not the first time that Nita has given up even before starting. This has happened on several occasions earlier and getting cold feet has become a habit for Nita. She is worried but has a hope that there is some support waiting for her on the other side of the gates, a new life, probably a successful one. She has a worried look on her face as she looks at the red brick building facing her, its massiveness leaves her flustered as she sees herself as a minute creature being crushed by its vastness. She is overpowered by fear as she looks at the huge building and her mind goes through various nightmares at great speed. She imagines seeing the building grow horns and large hands which move towards her to engulf her being. She panics and gasps for breath but Mini pulls her by her hand and takes her inside walking through the lawns to the red building. Nita looks around the campus which is very beautifully laid out and the landscape of the garden in front gives it an air of freshness that makes Nita feel a little comfortable.

They follow the arrows to the administrative office and reach a door marked "Principal". Nita freezes again and stares at the door for a few minutes before Mini gives her a strange look and nudges her to step into the Principal's office. "Don't you think we should meet someone in the administration office first?" Nita asks Mini who agrees and they look for the clerk who handles admissions. The room is vacant and they are not able to find any staff there so they assume that it might be a holiday for the staff today and decide to go to the Principal's office instead. Nita gathers her wits and walks into a huge chamber that almost looks like a library with bookshelves lining three sides of the room. She looks up at the tall roof of the chamber and moves around taking a three sixty degree view of the room that interests her due to its stained glass dome roof which has beautiful motifs etched in it lighting the chamber beautifully with various hues. The Principal, Mrs. Choudhary is an old, dignified and gentle lady who welcomes them and makes them feel comfortable and this puts Nita at ease. She looks through the Principal while she talks to her about the personality development classes like reciting a rehearsed poem without any expressions or punctuation marks. It is a tried and tested technique which helps Nita talk to people without getting edgy from noticing the frowns and smirks on their faces, just look through them and pretend they do not have an existence. Mrs. Choudhary is a different and a strange person as she does not frown at Nita and this is reason enough for Nita to feel that she must be dreaming as she has never faced such a nice person before who has not made fun of her or smirked at her. Mrs. Choudhary asks her to fill up some forms and tells her that she is lucky as she is just in time for the new session which is about to begin in the next fifteen minutes. "My admission clerk is on leave, I will ask someone else to help you with these forms," Mrs. Choudhary tells Nita as she picks up her intercom to summon someone to her room. A middle aged man comes within seconds to Mrs. Choudhary's chamber and helps Nita with her admission formalities. Nita looks at Mini and smiles and says, "It was a good idea to come here, thanks." The man gives Nita an encouraging smile that boosts her morale as she feels comfortable and at ease. Nita fills in the forms with her trembling hands, pays the admission fee and is soon admitted to the class.

Nita feels good about enrolling in the class but is uncomfortable at the thought of meeting her classmates and being questioned by the teachers. She is scared at the thought of having to make presentations with eyes gaping at her from frowning faces of her classmates. She is terrified of making silly mistakes which could make her a laughing stock and make her feel like a misfit in this world. She again looks at Mini for encouragement with fear in her eyes. "I think you will do very well. I am confident you will walk out as a very different individual from here," Mini encourages Nita. Nita believes Mini and enters her class holding her breath. There are fifteen students seated in the class and Nita has a strange feeling that they are looking at her with ridicule in their eyes and broad smiles on their faces that look fake to her. Nita walks slowly to her seat as the other students greet her. She nods her head and responds to them in a soft voice and quickly settles down in her seat before anyone can talk to her.

The teacher comes in after a few seconds and Nita finds him very frightening as he has a huge built and speaks in a roaring voice which is very intimidating. Mr. Kumar, the teacher, introduces himself to the students and then asks each of the students to introduce themselves to the class. The students start giving their introductions one by one with Mr. Kumar nodding and letting his facial muscles turn into a smile as he listens to them with absolute interest. Nita is distraught waiting for her turn and hopes that Mr. Kumar would forget to ask her. The voices of the students echo in the background while Nita chants a prayer to her God asking Him to make Mr. Kumar forget that she exists in the room. She senses that she is sitting on the edge of a cliff, holding the rocks beneath her desperately trying to avoid falling off the cliff. Exactly seven minutes later Mr. Kumar asks Nita to introduce herself to the class, alas, God has not heard her prayers, she surmises she must not have been loud enough for God to hear her. Nita does not hear Mr. Kumar the first time, forcing him to roar, reminding her to speak up. Nita wakes up and returns from the precarious cliff to the class and looks around trying to comprehend the situation as her cliff has suddenly disappeared and she has landed on plain land within seconds of perching atop a cliff.

Nita gets up from her seat and freezes with her eyes stuck on the wall in front, her ears cutting off every sound in the background, with the students and their voices fading away slowly and the wall in front disappearing from her view as her mind tries to block every possible distraction from it and her thoughts are gathering courage to speak up but her words refuse to form shape into an intelligent sound. Her words are stuck in her throat and she almost chokes as she speaks with the sound of her heartbeat that is increasing like the siren of a police van chasing a criminal. She tries not to look at the students or Mr. Kumar and imagines that they do not exist and that she is standing alone in the room holding Mini's hand. One of the girls giggles as Nita tries to speak up and there is a grin on a boy's face which terrifies Nita stopping her from speaking up and she pauses abruptly. Mr. Kumar encourages Nita to speak. "It is not very difficult. You can tell us about your education, your family and probably about your likes and dislikes. We would like to know you better as we are going to be together for the next six months. Take your time, you can introduce yourself at the end of the class but we should do this before we leave for the day," Mr. Kumar tells Nita in a deep modulated voice in an effort to make her comfortable. Nita is intimidated and breathes heavily before she makes another attempt to introduce herself to the class. Mini tries to encourage her by whispering in her ear, "Nita, we only have six months, you can do this with ease if you keep your cool and do not panic." Nita feels a little better with Mini's reassurance and continues to introduce herself. She manages to speak up but very timidly in a gentle soft voice which is loud enough to reach her ears alone. She has to clear her throat after every three words as her words have an unmatched and growing affinity for her larynx and remain glued to it for the fear of being heard by the world if they decide to flow out from her lips. Mr. Kumar thanks her and tells her to be louder in future, so loud that even the walls of the adjacent room are able to hear her voice. He glances at the class and begins the lesson for the day which comes as a respite to Nita as it means Mr. Kumar would not ask her to speak up again, at least till the end of the day. This is Nita's first class at the school and she tries hard to concentrate as Mr. Kumar walks them through the curriculum for the session and his expectations from the students and the schedule for evaluation tests to be held every fortnight. Nita can feel his voice piercing through her ear drums, a voice with a theatrical quality and a variety of modulations and expressions laying stress on every word that he speaks. "It is tough to sit here with all eyes on me," Nita tells Mini. "It is just fine, you are doing well, it is just a matter of a few hours and then we can move out, just try to hold on for some more time, we need to make it through the six months else you know....," Mini tries to motivate and comfort Nita. Nita's life is working through its design to bring her closer to the brightest colours of her soul, her highest potential and the sole aim with which her soul has taken birth in Saloni. The designs of life are only best known to the designer, the God, who has charted the path of life very well for each one of us and Nita has just begun her journey on the path designed for her. "Thanks Mini, what would I do without you," Nita smiles at Mini as she thanks her for her support. Raja, the student sitting on her right looks around as he sees Nita smiling at the wall on her side and Nita notices a strange confused look on his face making her immediately turn to her file on her table. She looks on her left and smiles again at Mini as Raja looks at her confused and disoriented as he can neither see the person she is talking to nor the one she is smiling at, which leaves him totally puzzled. Raja spends the entire class looking at

Nita who grins at the wall and talks to herself at times and even cups her hand on her mouth to whisper to the wall on her left; a behaviour which is very strange and confusing that Raja is unable to comprehend leaving him staring at Nita in his bewilderment.

Chapter 3

Aman is sitting on his favourite bench at the Maxing Garden overlooking Aseem Mountains, admiring the trees and imagining a painting of the beautiful landscape that he is beholding. He looks beyond the trees to the mountains and the skies and is suddenly reminded of the altercation at his home in the morning which has brought him here to get away from the problems of his life that haunt him all the time. His father had made him realize that he is 'good for nothing', which of course was not the first time in recent years that he had been confronted by this remark from his father as his repeated failures instigate his father to lose his temper and admonish him. He had taunted him about his inability to finish his management course and the strange ability to hop from one job to the other at a weekly frequency causing embarrassment to him. Aman's face turns pale as he thinks of his failures that have been too many in the recent months making his self-esteem slide to its lowest point and of course it is not unusual for Aman to feel so low as it is becoming an ingrown habit for him. He looks through the trees to the skies crowning the mountains with an emptiness in his eyes which is symbolic of his life, a meaningless journey through time which is treading towards oblivion like a withering plant breathing its last, the fading sun saying goodnight to the world as it recedes to another world. He too is slowly receding into his shell with the shades of dusk covering his face trying to hide his fears and worries in their dark folds. His perception of life is as dull as it can be, a world of the unknown mysteries hiding all meaning and purpose from him. He sees life to be very slow paced and filled with darkness making him a 'nobody' in the midst of the huge population of the surrounding world of achievers and super achievers. Aman looks at the white clouds turning black and disappearing with the sunlight like the various opportunities that come up in his life but fade away as quickly as they appear like little bubbles floating on the surface of sparkling water before they bid farewell to the world from a life of a few seconds. He looks around and bids goodbye to the trees and decides to leave for his home like birds who flock on their flight home after a long struggle filled arduous journey of the day. He gives the garden another look and sees himself stroking a canvas with his brush in an effort to paint the scenic beauty of the garden, his hands move with a flair of an experienced artist as he imagines the colours he has to use for his painting of the clouds, skies, trees and the mountains and his favourite bench which shares his worries and tensions and stands by him in every crisis as it defines the zone of his retreat from his failures. His faint smile soon vanishes as he remembers his father's harsh words from the argument in the morning, words that brought him face to face with reality, with his failures, with the uncertainty of his life's short-lived endeavours. He collects himself and decides to leave for his home as the moon begins to rise in the deep blue world of the skies to announce the arrival of another night.

Aman is another person who has not seen any colours of his soul till now and is considered a misfit, a slow learner and totally worthless by his parents, a concise definition of a person who is yet to set out in search of the brightest colours that correctly define the strength of his soul. A six feet tall, fair, rather handsome and well-built young man who is wandering in search of himself, lost and directionless as he moves across paths, climbs various hills but soon descends unable to find a strong foothold, grabs opportunities but gives up just when he starts, a soul set out on a voyage of self-discovery with a ship that wanders into unknown lands to add to his confusion. Aman studied in the most reputed boys' school and college before he studied Marketing at the Business School of Saloni, another reputed University of Saloni. He has been a hard working student and a lovable son but his limited attention span betrays his knowledge by diverting him to his passion for painting, a passion that breathes the elixir of life into him. He had given up the marketing course in the second year as it was uninteresting and unable to engage his focus bringing disappointment to his accomplished parents. His passion for painting keeps him busy with his brushes and paints which are his best friends as they bring out his innermost feelings on canvas with ease as his brush covers the canvas with different shades of colours to paint the songs of his soul, themes from his life's struggle, his dilemmas about his life and dreams of another world which is carefree. He could not remember to complete his homework when in school but never forgot to make a sketch as that was his favourite pastime and his passion, his devotion that emerged like a prayer on his sketchbooks and canvases that he made with great dedication. He had been caught sketching in class several times by his teachers who would call his parents to school making them feel embarrassed which in turn caused Aman to give up his playtime as his punishment for prioritizing his passion over his studies. Life for Aman has been limited to his paintings and to his childhood friend Ravi who is his support system, being there for him whenever there is any need. His love for his art keeps him home bound with little time for his friends and parents but he has a lifetime for his paintings which keep him totally engrossed as he sketches, colours and paints his creations that have the themes that can touch hearts and are highly thought provoking and intense matching the depth of his feelings. His world is limited to his room where he can spend the whole day moving his brush on his canvas to create magic with his colours to even give life and meaning to inanimate objects. Ravi is a regular visitor to his room who can sit with him for hours and talk to him at length as he watches him paint and add one more canvas to the portfolio of his creativity. He was always found in the lawns of his college campus where he sketched for hours and his presence in his class was a rare feature. Ravi would cover for him whenever the need arose and saved him many times from facing reprimand. Aman is a man of another time walking through this life as though lost in a dream trying to finish the time of this life in an aimless journey with no sight of an objective or the motivation of an ambition making his father comment on it as a 'waste of his life'. Aman's canvas brightens his life as it brings out his cheerful self, an absolutely different person who can give meaning to illusions with a stroke of his brush. He has won many prizes in school and college for his art but nothing for his studies but it does not create any need for concern as he is lost in his own world of colours. His works are enchanting when he puts his heart and soul in them, they speak and come alive and have a world of their own, a very different world which does not need degrees or jobs but just a contentment that arises from supreme creativity which exudes effortlessly from Aman's brush when he paints and sketches.

Chapter 4

The day is closing and sees Nita return home with Mini and sneak into the hideout of her room tiptoeing like a swift cat to avoid facing her parents about the travel business. She searches her bookshelf for her favourite book and slides into her chair with it to mark an end to a fruitful day. "Life could not be better!" she tells Mini as she relaxes in the comfort of her room. "Did you notice the other students in the class, Mini? I was too scared to even look at them. I felt I was surrounded by monsters who were about to grab my throat and strangle me without any instigation. Thank God, we have returned home safe and in one piece from the class," Nita sums up her day to Mini in a cheerful voice. Nita's comfort of her room brings out her cheerful and chirpy self as she feels at ease in her room, her cocoon which gives her the shelter that she really needs and lets her escape from the tough outside world. Her room makes her comfortable as it lets her be who she is without the need to pretend or get frightened or hide from anyone. This room makes her confident as it cuts her off from the big bad world and lets her be the person that she is. Nita pretends to be a Princess in her room and orders her soft toys around who obey her orders seriously with complete dedication and conviction making her feel like a supreme leader, a person of great ability who can bring out the best from her people who comply with her orders with great respect, dedication and devotion. Nita talks to her soft toys and then with Mini and switches on her television to watch her favourite show, a cartoon show which makes her find solace watching silly tricks that make her laugh with their comical nuances. Nita and Mini are soon rolling on the bed watching a cartoon show that is making them hysterical with its slapstick comedy. "This is so funny Mini. I can't stop laughing and my stomach hurts from laughing so much. This is the best show we have ever watched, is'nt it Mini?" Nita asks Mini as she tries to throw herself back into her chair. Nita is tired from laughing so much that she slides like a sack into her rocking chair while Mini is still rolling on the bed in peals of laughter. "Mini, do you want some popcorn?" Nita asks Mini. "No, I think I am okay," Mini tells her as Nita thinks of calling the housemaid for some popcorn. "Mini, life seems to be taking an interesting turn now, I like the way Mr. Kumar teaches us with patience, engaging us through the class and making sure that each student understands what is being taught in the class. I also liked the way he remained calm even when I fumbled while speaking. I think this class will help us a lot," Nita tells Mini with confidence which is slowly trying to make its way into her personality.

"Are you there Nita? I can hear you? Are you talking to yourself again?" Kaya calls out to Nita from the foot of the staircase that leads to her hideout. Nita hears her mother and decides to hide from her and from her queries and covers her face with her book as she hears footsteps approaching her room. "I knew it was you? What are you doing here all by yourself? I need to speak to you now?" Kaya tells her assertively. "Yes, Mom, ...I am listening," Nita replies incoherently as she lifts herself up from her chair and walks up to her mother with her fears returning back to her and lining her face with worry. "So, what is your decision? When are you joining your new office? Your Dad has your office ready and we want you to take up the responsibility immediately. No questions asked, no excuses! We will always be around to help, so you have no reason to get worried," Kaya tells Nita stressfully. Nita has a myriad of emotions playing like an orchestra out of rhythm on her confused face which shows her disinterest in the business and in any discussion related to it and the fear of the unknown as she does not know what her mother might make her agree to. Nita knows her Mom is not going to take 'No' for an answer. She looks at Mini and thinks through her answer before letting her lips part to speak to her mother, a well thought out answer that should not hurt her mother and still keep her own peace intact, her mind races to hunt for an apt response and skates through the network of neurons and grey cells of her brains at jet speed triggering every nerve cell to wake up and help her devise and design her reply quickly before her mother can think of any alternate that might be worse than the one she is presently faced with. Her forehead is crouched up and her eyes intensely tensed up as she thinks through her answer again and opens up to her mother, "Mom, can you give me six months, just six months. I promise I will be ready to take on the travel agency and any other business that you want me to but please give me just six more months. It is May, just give me time till October and I will take up the business, please Mom, please," Nita looks at Kaya with her pleading eyes as she speaks to her and turns to wink at Mini. Kaya's facial expressions have changed from streaks of intense worry to a stream of questions to fluttering anxiety and anger and finally to extreme relief on hearing Nita's decision. "Fine, so you have time till October, but no extensions! I am taking your word for it and will try to convince your father. But hear me out for the last time, there will be no excuses after October, okay," Kaya announces her decision to Nita. Nita nods in agreement with signs of comfort showing on her face and the deal is finally closed and sealed with mutual consent. Nita heaves a sigh of relief as she slides back into her chair with her book and winks at Mini who is giggling by her side. "Stop giggling Mini. Do you find this funny? I am nervous like hell and all you can do is show me your teeth. I am going to throw my pillow at you if you don't stop. By the way, do you think I did the right thing by buying time till October? Our classes will be over by then and I am sure I will be a different and of course, a confident person by that time. I am so glad and relieved that Mom agreed to my suggestion and did not force me to take over the business immediately,…..feel so much at ease now,…..I hope I will be able to manage the course well and get what I have set out for," Nita looks at Mini for reassurance. Mini agrees and smiles at Nita. Nita feels a sense of accomplishment running through her nervous system which is beginning to give her the confidence that she will be able to achieve what she has set out for. It is a cake walk making her mother agree to her plan but the uncertainty of the result of these six months makes her anxious as she does not know what life has in store for her, a positive result would be most welcome but anything negative would rebound to status quo for her, life looks so uncertain and its designs well obscured from her at present.

Chapter 5

———◆▶✖◀◆———

Aman is back from the mystic garden to a life of recluse in a home of ulterior grandeur that masks all his abilities, capabilities and desires like a beautiful flower that attracts attention to its flowers leaving the buds unnoticed. His father Jagat Dutt and mother Sheela Dutt are renowned Physicians known all across Saloni and in the nearby towns. Their practice brings in abundant wealth and splendour that gives their home excess of material possessions but there is a room of 'want', a room where Aman's dreams and desires are waiting to find the right ground to bloom and prosper. Aman feels lost in this home of plenty as it is like a canvas which has been splashed with colours all over its existence but the painting still lacks a face, a body, a soul, a misfortune to be lifeless even with full colours of life adorning it! Jagat and Sheela have accumulated tremendous wealth over the years but their real treasure is their only son Aman, their true wealth but they feel disappointed with his lack of ambition and interest in life which leaves them worried.

Aman sets up a new canvas on his easel and tries to capture the image of the trees with the mountains in the backdrop and he closes his eyes to recall the image that he was admiring at the Maxing Garden and smiles on seeing the picturesque landscape which he is about to paint and give life to. His brush strokes the canvas with great ease like gentle music falling on the connoisseur's sharp ears but is unsuccessful in creating magic that Aman seeks to see in his paintings, his hands fail to capture the image that his mind sees with total clarity and he can see that his painting is incomplete and lacks the exact potion of life which he wants to recreate on his canvas. "You need more practice with your strokes and colours," Jagat tells Aman as he is walking into Aman's room. Aman looks disheartened at the canvas, a look of a bird whose nest has been damaged by the storm, desperation and miserable regret at not being able to recreate his imagination, a sense of failure that screams at him from his canvas. He faces his father to admit his failure, to admit to himself that life is not moving in the direction he would want it to steer to. "Yes, Dad, you are right, I too am not too happy with this painting. It is lacking the essence that I want to create on this canvas, I am unable to create what I see, my hands do not feel what my eyes see," Aman replies in a sad tone to his father as his mind wanders to the Maxing Garden, his inspiration for this painting. He is recreating the image of the garden in his mind but is unsuccessful, the mind looks at a beautiful picture but the heart is not able to make the hands translate it into a painting on his canvas, the finer details are blurred from his vision as he is disturbed by the events from the morning. His father can sense his feelings and wants to comfort him and make him realize that life needs a purpose and a job to sustain itself and Aman is nowhere close to finding any of them. "Do you think you can make a living by just moving your brush on a canvas?" Jagat questions Aman in an effort to comfort him but his tone of confrontation makes Aman feel worse as it shows him the mirror of his failures. "You will not be able to survive in this world by just sitting in your room with your brush and colours. You need much more that this to sail through your life Aman. Start thinking seriously about it. You neither have a goal in life, nor are you willing to think about it," Jagat speaks to Aman in a frustrated tone.

Sheela enters the room and senses the heat of the battle between her worried husband and her disheartened son and tries to ease the father son tension by asking them to join her for a game of chess, her favourite past time and an easy technique to divert attention from the issue at hand. Sheela asks Jagat to remain patient and wait for Aman to take life head on. Sheela understands her son and knows he has immense capabilities but he is not taking the lead to hold his life's reins. "Don't worry about Aman. He will soon find something that he can manage with interest and will make us proud, he has the potential but there is lack of willingness and focus that takes him to the doorstep of failure each time he tries to take some steps towards a new destination. Just wait and see he will surely do us proud, won't you Aman?" Sheela tries to calm Jagat's worries and looks at Aman for a reply. Jagat looks at her with a little hope, a hope that Sheela's faith may lead to some positive outcomes, a hope that Aman may settle down with a lucrative and sound job in his life, a hope that he will find his way through life to make a place for himself, a hope of a mother to see her son win. "Yes Mom, I will," Aman replies to his mother but there is a doubt in his mind and his heart flutters as he is unsure of honouring his commitment to his mother. The three of them move to the activity room as Aman ponders over his father's questions which are echoing in his mind and screaming at him and showing him the mirror which reflects the image of a person who has failed miserably in his life. He knows he does not have a goal in life and that makes him panic for the first time in his life as he sees himself stranded in the middle of the ocean with no sight of land till the farthest distance, like a shipwrecked man floating in the middle of nowhere. The game of chess keeps Aman and his parents busy for an hour before the Jagat Mansion passes into a deep slumber with the clock striking twelve to announce the arrival of midnight. Jagat Mansion is a grand villa in the uptown sprawling land of the exclusive Pawan Gardens near the Aseem Forest. An eight bedroom villa spread over two floors with a beautiful garden connecting the porch and the black iron gate of the villa. The driveway has tiles with a cobbled path designed to give it a rustic look. The interiors of the villa have an ornamental décor with the antique look furniture giving it a feel of royalty at its best. Sheela has got the mansion designed by the top architect of Saloni and she takes pride in her selection of the fittings, fixtures, furniture and linen that makes the mansion look regal.

Chapter 6

Nita is looking forward to the next morning to focus on the personality development course which will determine the fate of both the travel agency and her life. "Mini, I am really looking forward to the class, I will take a seat which is in the corner so that I am away from the rest of the students and get some privacy. I do not like the way Raja stares at me, it makes me uncomfortable," Nita tells Mini who is looking at her through her sleepy eyes. The stars in the sky are bright like a premonition of good times to soon appear on the horizon of her life to catapult her from her limitations to a confident self with immense capability to walk through the path of her life. She admires the stars from her window and falls asleep to dream of herself as a royal Princess with exceptional powers to make the world dance to her tunes, a world which does not know any negativity where she can be very confident without fearing anyone for mocking her. She spends the night smiling through her dreams and is woken up by the screams of the peacocks and the orange rays from the sun that are giving her eyes a golden hue, a sign of the golden times waiting ahead for her in life. She looks around for Mini and asks her to get ready to leave for their class at the Arts School.

Nita is greeted by Simi and Ajay at her class which comes as a surprise to her as she has never encountered such warmth and welcome feeling in her life till now, almost like an emotional outburst, an unexpected shower on a parched land that has been thirsty for ages, a significant event in Nita's life bringing a much needed boost for her low morale and self-esteem, a sense of achievement that leaves her as a conqueror of her limitations. "Hi Nita, I am Simi and he is Ajay. You must have seen us in the class yesterday. We were sitting right in front of you. You look so graceful and gentle that we want to be friends with you," Simi tells Nita as Ajay nods his head in confirmation.

Simi is a short bespectacled little girl with a cheerful personality who is forever smiling and Ajay is a stout and tall boy who has a serious disposition as he finds it difficult to smile and speak. Nita looks at them and smiles as she cannot believe what she has just heard and responds in her regular precise way, "Sure." She smiles at Mini and winks at her to let her know that she has finally had a breakthrough in life. Her joy has no bounds on knowing that Simi and Ajay find her graceful and gentle, the qualities that she thought only Mini could possess but are now hers too to her surprise. She has made two new friends and that makes her feel so proud and elated that she hops around the class in her joy of her latest accomplishment, like a small bird who has found its nest near the branch where it was searching for its home. Her happiness pours through her eyes and her smile making Ajay adore her, he keeps looking at her with admiration as she takes her seat. There is a sudden sharp comment from a classmate Dani that makes her smile fade away instantly like a dark cloud covering the face of the moon. Dani is a short and bald man who walks like a toddler and has the evil mind of a demon. "So this is Miss Mumble, hey why could'nt you speak up in the class yesterday. Miss Nervous!" Nita is used to hearing such statements since her childhood so she knows how to pretend not to be affected by the remarks at all, to have the knack to make her hearing selective and block the voices that cannot be gentle. She ignores him and takes her seat while Simi and Ajay flank her on the seats on her sides. "Just ignore him Nita, he is too mean to be given any importance," Simi tries to console Nita who is hurt but trying to keep a calm look on her face. "Yes, Simi is right Nita, just ignore him," Ajay adds to Simi's consolation as he looks at her dark brown eyes and dark brown hair and feels lost in her beauty. Nita nods her head and reminds herself that it is a matter of only six months and she can manage this time easily if she is focussed on the curriculum. She holds Mini's hand tightly as she is unable to respond to Dani and is hurt and there is a feeling of losing out in life to the wicked beings. Mini tries to calm her down as she asks her to count till ten and take a deep breath. Nita follows Mini's instructions diligently and feels a little better on counting till ten and taking a deep breath, the breath that tells her that it is the class that matters to her in life and everything else is immaterial, the deep gush of fresh air that enhances her focus and energizes her, bringing a renewed zest in her outlook towards her life. Simi and Ajay look around trying to see whom is Nita talking to but do not find anyone around so they give Nita a weird look that makes her uneasy. Nita smiles at them and faces the whiteboard near Mr. Kumar's table. Mr. Kumar makes an appearance soon and takes them through the course for the day.

Nita has her entire attention focussed on the lesson though her mind is running through the snide remarks made by ugly Dani, and Mini is trying her level best to comfort Nita with her efforts to divert her attention to the lesson. Mr. Kumar asks the students to come up with a speech on a topic of current relevance and gives them fifteen minutes for preparation bringing the class to total attention with the students whispering to each other as they discuss the topics they would like to present and consult their peers for advice. "Each student will get ten minutes to talk," Mr. Kumar announces and this has Nita all worked up. The thought of facing the class and especially Dani is nerve wrecking as she gulps and clenches her fists in an attempt to control her nervousness. She tries to gather her courage and thinks through the topic while there are unsettled questions at the back of her mind as she has to look confident and appear normal under all circumstances. She thinks about talking on the environment and the importance to conserve resources which has become a pressing problem with the increasing growth in population globally. She quickly jots down some points and arranges them into sentences and has her speech ready within a few minutes and starts to revise the details. She is an intelligent person with a great flair for writing and the gross inability to speak in public. She tries to look into her paper that brings her comfort from the terrifying thought of facing Mr. Kumar but Mr. Kumar senses her apprehension and calls out her name first, giving her a nervous shock and making her hands shiver as she tries to walk up in front of the class holding on to her paper like a snail crawling onto a branch and curling around it to avoid slipping into the puddle of water at the foot of the plant. Mini taps her shoulder to boost her confidence and says to her, "Nita, just kill it! You can and you will". Nita nods her head at Mini and recites her prayers in her mind and decides to outdo herself and starts reading out from her paper as words fall out gently from her lips in a constant flow but she forgets to add expression in her hurry to read the speech and get away with it reducing the impact of her beautiful speech. Mr. Kumar lets her complete her speech without any interruption before he gives her his assessment of the content, presentation and confidence. He explains to her and to the class how Nita could have projected the speech to have an instant hit with her audience and encourages Nita to face the world with extreme confidence. "Confidence needs to be built from within. Nita, you know your subject and have the expertise and a gifted flair to sum it up in words. You need to be louder and assertive and not project yourself as a weak, terrified soul who is unsure of herself. You will be making another presentation tomorrow morning on a topic of your choice and this time I want to see you more assertive and confident and of course, not reading out from a paper," Mr. Kumar tells Nita as she keeps nodding her head in agreement. Nita is terrified at the thought of having to present to the class again but tries to calm her nerves and tells herself that she will be confident and make an effective presentation though her heart is thumping with terror as she thinks of how she will face the class again tomorrow morning. She notices Dani's smirk and that is sufficient reason to trigger terror and nervousness in her but she remembers the advice from Simi and Ajay and takes a deep breath to relieve her tension and build her confidence. Mini holds her hand and tells her not to look at Dani. "You did well Nita, this was really good, I have never heard you speak so well before, this was just fine," Mini tells Nita. Nita is hurt by Dani's behaviour but tries not to get influenced by it making her decide to prove to the class and to herself that she can face the class and speak with total confidence. She prays to God for strength and courage to make an effective speech without any intimidation from her classmates. "Mini, you are right, I will not worry about anything else, people like Dani are destructive and do not matter as they will never allow me to build my positivity and my confidence. I have to let go of my nervousness and insecurities to face such people and face life," Nita declares her decision to Mini in a mumble. Simi and Ajay are staring at Nita to figure out whom is she talking to but are unable to which leaves them thoroughly confused. "Whom are you talking to?" Simi whispers to Nita. "Mini, I was talking to Mini," Nita replies. "Who?" Simi asks in her bewilderment. "Mini,.........I mean no, ...I mean nobody," Nita replies realizing that Simi does not know Mini. There is a strange look on Simi's face as she turns to look at Ajay who too is in a confused state of mind as Nita has a weird habit of talking to herself or to the wall on her side frequently and this leaves them totally intrigued.

Nita returns home contented after delivering the speech though with some lapses but it still brings a smile on her face as she senses some improvement in her confidence level. She is hopeful of honouring her commitment to her mother and that makes her happy with herself. "Mini, it was a good day at the school today, wasn't it?" Nita asks Mini. Mini is busy reading something and does not pay much attention to Nita but nods her head, an acknowledgement of whatever that she might be saying as Mini's approval uplifts Nita's spirits. "I think it was surely a good idea to join the class, thanks for the suggestion Mini, it was a great one, I am sure the classes are going to help us a lot, don't you think so Mini? Nita questions Mini again. Mini looks up from her book peeping at her with her dark brown eyes and nods again, "Yes, it was a good idea and things will move well from now onwards," Mini tells her with her eyes returning to the book she is reading. "I am looking forward to the next lessons, I will try to improve my presentation next time and give that ugly Dani no chance to pass any remarks at me," Nita says in her excitement and bites her lip. "Mini, can I read my speech to you and you can give me your feedback on my presentation?" Nita asks Mini. "Okay, sure go ahead," says Mini and Nita starts her speech. It is a long speech and Nita has her expression and pauses just right for her speech which make it sound very effective and leave Mini thoroughly impressed. Each word of her speech is like a stepping stone leading her to her goal and adding to her confidence with each step that she climbs bringing joy and pride in Mini's eyes that are glowing with Nita's progress and betterment. Mini claps and praises her, "Bravo, that was great, I am sure Mr. Kumar is going to be very impressed with you this time, just wait and see, he will be singing praises for you and that Dani will have no chance to make fun of you." Nita feels good hearing Mini out and is confident of managing her speech well in the next class. "What would I do without you Mini? You are an angel who is always there to support me," Nita appreciates Mini's help and the two of them settle on the couch to watch their favourite show on television.

Chapter 7

Aman has quit his latest job, a regular pattern in his life now, so it leaves him unperturbed as he has reached a stage of complacence where the availability of a job or its absence has stopped having any effect on him. He decides to return to Maxing Garden and celebrate his latest failure in the shade of the Magnolia trees lining the picturesque mountains in the distance.

He calls up his friend to give him the news, "Ravi, I have quit my job, I could not carry on with it, my attention span is too limited for a desk job, can't keep my focus on numbers and accounts, I am not made for it. Don't know how Mom and Dad will react when they get to know. They are already very cross with me." Aman takes a deep breath as he talks to Ravi. "Where are you and what are you doing right now Aman?" asks Ravi. "I am at the Maxing Garden trying to hide away from the world," Aman tells Ravi in a low sounding indifferent tone, a tone that defines that the limit of his tolerance has been breached and he has reached a dead end, an impasse that offers him no option but to reverse the wheels of his life and he does not know where he should go after he reverses from the cul-de-sac of his life. "Okay, I will be there in thirty minutes," Ravi tells Aman. Aman gets up from the bench and takes a stroll in the garden as he waits for Ravi to show up with his mind restless and his heart unable to decide what is right for him, what will see him settle down with a job or a business capable of supporting his existence and helping him avoid embarrassment to his parents which he feels is most important as his parents have built a high reputation for themselves with their flourishing practice and expertise in their field and he does not want to do anything that would maim their respect in society in any way. He has not been able to find out what his true potential is and that is constantly frustrating him, making him restless and torn as he sees himself locked in a dungeon which does not have any doors or windows and there is not a single ray of hope to guide him through his darkness. He is unsure of the job that would make him happy, something that will help him continue in a job with complete focus and good interest and give him a purpose to carry on, an aim for his life that would give meaning to his existence. It is a moment of total darkness in his life where he is left groping for support.

Ravi comes after half an hour and punches him in his belly. "So Aman, gave it up again," Ravi says in a casual tone to bring Aman back from his deep rooted thoughts. "Yes, did it again," Aman sighs and looks at the skies. "I am as blank as the skies right now. Don't know what to do? I am clueless like a lost bird desperately trying to search for a branch to rest on, these jobs are too boring and drain me out, I do not seem to find any interest in a desk job, I had tried a marketing job too and that turned out to be as dull and boring as a desk job, I am not made for working in an office where I am tied down with work that does not make much sense to me and fails to evoke my interest," Aman remarks in his frustration. Ravi and Aman walk through the garden to the nearby swimming pool while Ravi is thinking of various ways to help his friend. They take the chairs near the pool and order for some snacks while Aman's mind is flowing haphazardly through the streets of Saloni in search of an answer to unknown questions leaving him in absolute frustration. Ravi's mind is working overtime to find a solution to Aman's problems and his eyes are watching the swimmers splashing in the pool. He suddenly notices a person emerging out of the pool and recognizes him instantly. "The man is a champion now, all he did was turn his passion for swimming into his profession and now he is swimming for the State, can you believe that and,…….. if he can, so can you, me, we and why not?" Ravi speaks out in a single breath in his excitement as Aman looks at him trying to comprehend his statement. "Yes, we too can Aman. We definitely can do it too. Aman, just think of something you would really like to do, something that brings out the best in you, your passion, your creativity, anything that you just love to do and can do twenty four by seven without getting bored or tired of it," Ravi asks Aman in an excited voice and looks at him earnestly for a quick response. "You know, I, for instance can sleep for the whole day or watch cricket for hours. I don't need to work as I get sufficient rental income from my properties. If I really had to work I would just do something that lets me watch cricket all my life. You know, like being a commentator or something," Ravi adds on. Aman looks at Ravi and tries to understand his point of view. Aman looks at the skies and smiles and sees himself in front of an easel drawing a sketch. "I would really like to be an artist, a painter who can spend his entire life painting," Aman declares and realizes that with this remark he has unknowingly discovered what he likes doing the best, he has been suddenly struck by lightning that has brought him face to face with the aim of his life, giving his life and his existence a purpose that has till now been faded and obliterated from his view. Painting has always been a passion that brings out the best in Aman as his prime thought on beholding anything is a brush stroke that can translate what he sees into a story through paints splashed meaningfully across a canvas. Yes, it is painting that sums up Aman's character, his personality, his soul, his aim in life and Aman smiles as he has accidentally discovered himself, his face glows with the realization and his eyes smile as they look up to the clear skies in acknowledgement of his discovery. He wants to thank Ravi for helping him explore his true potential and identify the exact purpose of his life, the floodgates seem to have been opened with this thought and he is standing amidst an ocean of peace and happiness with his feet being tickled by the sand particles that are moving away from under his feet with the flow of water as he stands on the beach drawn on the canvas of his life.

He looks at Ravi with a smile beaming across his handsome face but Ravi is engrossed in thinking how he can help Aman. "So why don't you take up painting as a profession?" Ravi questions him. "May be I could, but there is a hitch as I have yet to perfect many techniques," Aman tells Ravi as he ponders over his question in deep thought. "So go ahead and perfect them," Ravi makes life so simple for Aman by making this simple statement. "But how?" asks Aman. "You could ....take lessons ....or join some classes, ...find a mentor, a teacher, ...maybe take up painting classes at the Arts School," Ravi suggests instantly. Ravi is convinced that the answer lies in the Arts School so he forces Aman to join the painting class at the Arts School. The failures in Aman's life have driven him to his heart's desire and are unfolding the doors of his life to discover his true passion for painting.

The thought of joining the Arts School has come as a desirable option and Aman just cannot wait till the next morning to get enrolled in the Arts Class for honing his painting skills. He has accidentally viewed the hues of his soul through the design of life that has brought him to his own spectrum of colours with repeated failures in the path of his life, like a person who constantly takes the wrong roads and wrong turns and returns to the start point each time in frustration but he tries again and again till he eventually drives to the right destination. He cannot sleep in his excitement of going to the class and learning the skills that will take him straight to his dreams and passion and add valuable meaning to his purposeless and aimless life. There is a ray of hope finally that is lighting up his darkness with hopes and expectations from his decision to join the class.

The next morning begins with a promise to open new doors in Aman's life as he walks into the Arts School and enrolls himself for the painting class. He strolls around the campus to get a feel of the surroundings that will see him emerge as an artist in the true sense. He walks up to his teacher with great confidence as he sees in him a mentor who is about to raise his magic wand and place him next to achieving his passion, like a click of a mouse that clicks and drags an image from a point to the other on a computer screen. Aman is looking forward to the click that will open a new screensaver for him on the laptop of his life. Mr. Sharma asks Aman in his squeaky voice to paint something on a small canvas to assess his current skills, to identify his present potential and the gaps and shortfalls which he can help him overcome with refined techniques. Aman takes the test and paints a swing on the branch of a beautiful tree which seems to have just been vacated by someone after swinging on it for some time as it is still in motion with its ropes flowing back towards the tree. Mr. Sharma admires his strokes and can see that his painting has a life and a soul which speak out from the colours of the canvas and there is a small distance that he needs to cover from his excellent art form to making a master piece. His balding head speaks of the many decades he has spent in perfecting the techniques of various types of art forms that now gives him the advantage to share his rich experience with others. He picks up a brush and refines the painting with a few colours and strokes of the brush that moves on the canvas like a beautiful wave in a calm mood that clears the sands of footprints to give it a new and fresh look. Aman admires his teacher's work and they discuss and practice some techniques through the day. Aman feels fortunate to have found a great teacher who will make him excel in his passion, someone who will help him achieve what he has set out for with his support and inspiration. He is motivated to draw another sketch which he starts working on immediately with his hand moving in waves to infuse life into his canvas.

Mr. Sharma is speaking to Pam about her glass painting. Pam is another student who has come to learn some techniques for stain glass art. Pam is a lean and fit girl with short hair and small eyes that have a habit to look sideways. Pam notices Aman's sketch and is drawn towards it as it is too beautiful and she is unable to take her eyes off the painting though her eyes have envy masked in them. Mr. Sharma follows Pam and they are both intrigued by the magnificent lake with mountains in the backdrop and dark clouds lining the skies that are being perfected by Aman with the tip of his brush. Mr. Sharma picks up a brush and refines the lines of the lake as Aman's eyes move in line with the brush to understand the gaps in his art that his teacher is trying to fill with his superior knowledge and experience. Pam stands behind them in admiration of the painting and a frown on her face that suggests jealousy. Mr. Sharma appreciates Aman's work and his admiration brings out the green colour of envy from Pam who is jealous of hearing her teacher admire someone else's art form. Mr. Sharma asks Aman to draw a human figure as he wants to see his skills on that front too. He also asks Pam and Aman to exchange notes on their art forms and meet other students in the class. This is a class of six students with Mr. Sharma as their main teacher. Each student is an artist in the making with expertise in varied skills and art forms.

Aman moves his brush swaying it across his canvas bringing out the colours of sand on the beach and then he draws a man and a woman walking on the beach with high tide waves receding on the side. The silhouettes of the man and woman slowly come alive as he paints them with perfection. It is a painting of two souls trying to walk through their lives together and facing every challenge that life brings forth in its wake. Aman steps back to see his creation and wonders if he will ever find a partner who will walk with him through the challenges of life and share his happiness too. Mr. Sharma spends a long time assessing the sketch and mentions the need to adhere to proportions while drawing such figures and asks him to rework on the painting. Aman finds the class soul-satisfying as it totally engrosses him in his passion bringing a constant smile on his face as he works on his paintings like a musician playing the violin, his brush moves like the bow on strings of life and creates the soul of music with varied shades of colours and myriad brush strokes that move on the canvas in a divine dance.

Chapter 8

Simi, Ajay and Nita are having some snacks at the canteen of the Arts School where they meet students from other courses. Nita feels comfortable in Simi and Ajay's company and is at ease in the cafetaria even though there are a good number of people present in the canteen around her. Simi and Ajay introduce Nita to their friends from the pottery class. Nita is happy to meet these friends as they are very warm and devoid of any intentions of mocking her. Nita wonders if people are changing their behaviour towards her or if she has undergone any change in her perceptions and outlook towards people. She is confused and lacks clarity so she looks at Mini with multiple questions in her eyes that give them a puzzled look. Mini knows her problem instantly and tells her very softly, "Your confidence is growing and that is making you look at people without any pre-conceived notions about them. Your fears of people ridiculing you will drop as you gain confidence in yourself. These classes are helping you out and Simi and Ajay are also instrumental in boosting your morale and infusing you with confidence with their friendship and trust in you." Nita knows Mini has to be right so she nods her head in affirmation and smiles at Ajay and Simi. She feels fortunate to have found such good friends like Simi and Ajay who have been able to help her when she needed it the most, like an anchor that prevents her from drowning in her bewilderment and anxiety that emanate from her nervousness. Simi tells Nita she has to meet her father before she leaves for the day. "Why don't you come with me to my father's class? He is a teacher in this school," Simi asks Nita and Ajay to accompany her. Simi takes them to the next wing in the campus. This is a part of the campus unknown to Nita and Ajay. They walk through the corridors to Simi's father's class.

Mr. Sharma is surprised to see Simi. "Simi, are you not going home? When did your class get over?" Mr. Sharma asks Simi. "I am about to leave Papa, I was with my friends….we were having a snack…I need some money…. and these are my friends Nita and Ajay." Mr. Sharma smiles at Nita and Ajay and hands over some cash to Simi. The three of them look around the class and admire the paintings pinned on the board, the artwork of some of the students. Nita is fascinated by the painting of a man and woman walking on the beach and she stands there in admiration with her eyes glued to the painting and she is unable to hear anything round her. She asks Mr. Sharma about the artist and expresses her desire to meet him. Mr. Sharma calls Aman and introduces him to Nita, Simi and Ajay. "He is the artist who has made this beautiful painting and there are some more of his creations on the board outside the class. Why don't you show them your work, Aman?" Aman is extremely happy to meet admirers of his work and takes them to the board in the corridor outside the class. Nita looks at his paintings with great admiration and Simi and Ajay also appreciate his paintings making Aman swell with pride. Aman is overjoyed to hear Nita talk about his work as she is able to go into the details of his painting and appreciate the use of colours, the delicate strokes, the shades used, the depth of the theme, the underlying concept and the superlative impact of the overall composition of his work.

Nita walks from one painting to the next and scans every painting in detail till she reaches the last one and stands mesmerized with her eyes fixed on it as she is transported to a dream land with its incredible theme. Aman looks at her and wonders what her reaction would be as he has been hearing beautiful comments from her for all his works and this one is special for him and he waits anxiously for her reaction with his heart beating loudly in anticipation of listening to positive feedback about his work. Nita takes a while before she comments on his last painting bewitched with its charisma, lost in its captivating theme and totally engrossed in its beauty. "These two souls look so much in love and are walking together all the way through their lives, their togetherness is so meaningful as they hold their hands and look at life and its challenges in the waves that they are facing together. This is such a beautiful painting, Aman. Just see their shadows behind them as though they are coming out of their shadows in search of light, a new life, success and the truth of their existence as they walk into shining bright light," Nita gives Aman her interpretation of his painting as her eyes are sparkling in awe of its beauty that leaves Aman in wonder and he cannot help but admire Nita. She has summed up his work so well which was impossible even for him to do, a beautiful description of his work that has magnified its worth and has given a new definition to his art. It is the first time in his life that he has met a true admirer of his work who understands his creativity and shares the zeal for his passion with an equal intensity as his. Nita is very impressed by his work and finds him to be a great artist who has a very bright and successful future carved for himself as she finds his paintings very remarkable as they have a high degree of meaning in them and they seem to have a soul that makes them breathe life and makes them appear larger than life. She shares her thoughts with Aman and that makes Aman feel immensely satisfied with his work and is grateful for hearing her talk with so much positivity about his work.

"Mini, is this not the best work you have ever seen in your life?" Nita asks Mini. Mini nods in agreement. "Did you say something to me?" Aman asks Nita. "No, I was talking to Mini," Nita replies instantly. "Mini, who is Mini?" Aman asks her. She is left gaping and turns towards Aman's painting and says, "No, nothing, ...nobody." Aman is confused by her remark but tries not to continue with the conversation and changes the topic to the weather, a favourite topic that can be handled with utmost ease at any time.

Aman and Nita soon become great friends and Nita sees her circle of friends expanding to include Simi, Ajay and Aman. Pam comes up to meet Simi and her friends and they learn from her some basic information on stain glass art. Pam shows them her work and Nita finds her to be showing off her work in order to score one up on Aman and this puts off Nita who still appreciates the effort that she has put in her work. Simi and Ajay also tell Pam that they like her work though their facial expressions do not match their words of praise. Her work is good but not excellent but she is hankering for the same level of appreciation that Aman is getting for his work. Nita finds it unfair for people to seek results that are much more than the effort they put in their work. Aman introduces them to the other students in his class Deep, Vijay, Rahul and Sunita. They look through the paintings made by Deep and Rahul and the sand art paintings of Vijay and Sunita and find them very beautiful and inspiring with their varied themes that are based on the present day problems of hunger and poverty being faced by the world at large. Nita leaves with her friends in some time and tells Aman to call her when he finishes his next piece of art. "Call me when it is ready, I would like to see it and I would like to see each and every one of your paintings as I find them extraordinary," Nita tells Aman. "Sure, I will, I am happy that you like my work," Aman replies with a sense of jubilation and achievement as his work has found great words of appreciation and admiration. Aman has never encountered so much happiness in his life as his work has now found a real life with a purpose and this makes him overjoyed!!

Aman returns home in a very lively and energetic mood with happiness pouring through his soul and his eyes beaming with joy as he has found a true friend and a genuine admirer of his work which motivates him to paint more and more. He starts creating a new story on a new canvas, a very different artwork this time, a piece of art that talks of happiness and optimism in its bold colours and shades. His efforts and creativity double up as he wants to make something new to show Nita, his true admirer. He is going through every detail over and over again as he wants greater admiration for his work this time. His brush strokes are as smooth as silk and as exact as perfection and the shades of the colours he is using reflect his inner happiness and peace lending a life and soul to his work that speaks to those who see it. Jagat is surprised to see Aman so engrossed in his work for the first time in his life as he does not even feel his father's presence in his room. "Your painting seems to talk and I can sense joy in it," Jagat recognizes Aman's work for the first time. Aman looks at Jagat with great surprise and disbelief as Jagat has never appreciated his work till now, making his happiness grow manifold on hearing his father's positive comments about his work. "Thanks Dad. I am so glad that you like it," Aman says with delight. "Yes, it is beautiful. I must show it to Sheela too. She will be impressed on seeing her son's creation." He calls out to Sheela and as expected Sheela looks at the sketch in awe and stands speechless in front of the easel. "It is really beautiful. How did you make it Aman? This is the first time you have made something that looks like a piece of art. Wow! God bless you son!" Sheela says with tears in her eyes. Aman's joy knows no bounds and he thinks of Nita and thanks her in his thoughts for bringing out the best in him. The compliments from his parents are like an unexpected shower on a sunny day that leave him drenched in happiness, a feeling of extreme joy on being appreciated by them for the first time in his life, bringing contentment and peace to the ripples of his frustration with himself. His smile speaks of the intensity of his happiness that has been brought by an achievement which he had never expected to reach in his life and the realization, that he would not turn into an embarrassment for his parents, enhances his joy. Jagat Mansion is in a celebratory mood after a long time with Jagat, Sheela and Aman enjoying their match of chess together as they talk at length about their day's events. Jagat and Sheela are overjoyed to hear about Aman's successful ventures at his class and are happy for his achievement as they can see a ray of hope trickling into their life.

Nita also returns in a happy mood as she has found new friends and has appreciated Aman's work. The feeling that grows within after appreciating someone is just beyond all joy one can get from watching a rainbow appear in the sky, it is a feeling of extreme elation that reflects through her soul and her gestures as she hops around her home humming a sweet tune. She is so impressed by Aman's work that she wants to see more of it and she keeps thinking of the paintings she has seen during the day. She talks at length with Mini about Aman's paintings and their varied themes that caught her fascination, the immense power of his paintings that captivates her making her want to see more of his work. She is awed with Aman's work and is upset with Pam who behaved like a small child who was seeking attention for her work, "Or was she jealous of Aman's skills?" Nita thinks aloud. Kaya and Shan are happy to see their daughter in a fairly good mood. She is not her usual self today and that makes their home Ashiana find a reason to celebrate. Shan asks Kaya if they should go out for dinner and Kaya finds it a great idea and the three of them leave for their favourite restaurant.

Kaya and Shan are relieved to see their daughter in a good mood with signs of confidence in her approach to things. The initial signs of her growing confidence peek through her mannerisms as she orders her favourite dishes without shuffling through the menu card or looking around for an imaginary person to exchange notes on the menu and relishes her food with great happiness that reflects in her constantly beaming smile. They exchange silent and happy glances on seeing their daughter enjoying her dinner, a divine solace from the confidence that is building up in Nita. The day is meeting an apt closure and Nita and Aman are looking forward to the next morning with intense curiosity and great expectations, Nita's curiosity to meet Aman to see his creations and expectations of beholding a masterpiece and Aman's curiosity to know what Nita thinks of his work and his expectations of getting good comments from her. Life has suddenly brought two people of diverse natures together to help them discover themselves, explore their extreme potentials and taste the success of life!! Life has definitely got its delightful designs and knows how and when to execute them!! The chirping of birds greets the next morning as the brightness of the sun seems to enlighten it with the knowledge of the new day that seems to turn the clock in a new direction. "Mini, we need to leave soon, I cannot wait to see what Aman has painted today," Nita tells Mini anxiously with great excitement in her voice. Mini looks at her with a smile and says, "I have never seen you like this before, you seem to be changing, Nita." "Yes, I think I am changing. There is some invisible power in Aman that makes me run to him," Nita replies.

Chapter 9

Nita is ready with her speech and is gathering courage to speak in front of the class with full confidence but she cannot wait for her class to be over and get a chance to run to the other wing of the campus and adore Aman's paintings while Aman is busy perfecting his new painting before he can show it to Nita, a strange cord connects them in an unusual way. This painting seems to link Aman and Nita into a bond of true friendship as its colours enhance their joys and its theme captivates their soul.

Mr. Kumar takes up a small session on grooming and its effect on personality for the class before he asks Nita to deliver her speech. Nita is a different person this morning and Mini, Simi and Ajay have also told her so and this confirmation has raised her hopes about her success for the day and that brings a little confidence in her stride. "All the best Nita," Mini wishes her good luck before she gets up to speak. She avoids looking at Dani and starts to speak. She has memorized her lines well and the words seem to flow out from her well defined lips gently but effectively. The degree of her nervousness has declined but she is still not totally confident so she speaks out like a robot, totally expressionless, just a stream of words being poured into a vessel in an endeavour to get rid of them as fast as she possibly can. Mr. Kumar thanks her and appraises her, stressing on the need for expressions while talking to give life to her words and transfer their meaning and intended purpose to her listeners. He appreciates the improvement in her over the last class which makes her feel relieved but his comments on her expressions leave her with a huge scope to better her presentation skills. Ajay is the next speaker for the day who starts talking as Nita takes her seat.

Nita is not listening to his speech as she is thinking about her improving confidence that is showing in her glowing persona and of Aman's splendid creations which have left her in total awe, her physical presence in the class conceals her mental and emotional absence from it beautifully as her frowns and smiles camouflage her thoughts and intentions of rushing out of the class. "Can't wait to rush out to meet Aman," Nita tells Mini in her excitement. Her eyes are moving from Mr. Kumar to her file and then to her watch in succession with continuous repetition in the same sequence till the end of the class while her heart is singing a new song, a strange sensation which is new for Nita. Nita rushes to Aman as soon as her class is over to find him totally engrossed in perfecting his new painting. Nita is amazed to see the wonderful piece of work which Aman has created especially for her. It is a superb depiction of the rising sun from behind the dense trees and over the silvery waters of the ocean. The painting looks so real that Nita cannot stop admiring it as she goes close to the canvas and remarks on the use of various shades of yellow, gold and silver and the three dimensional feel of the cobbles under the water. She surprises Aman with her knowledge of colours and her insights into this art form. "Did your teacher like this painting? What was his reaction? Did he comment on the colours?" Nita asks Aman excitedly. "Yes, he liked it, he found it to be almost a masterpiece but still not My Masterpiece," Aman tells Nita with a hint of disappointment in his voice which reaches Nita who feels sorry for him as his efforts have not met the desired level of appreciation that he expected and even she thought the painting to be worthy of. "You will surely have your masterpiece ready very soon Aman, I find this to be your masterpiece but he is a better judge and if he says so, we should believe him. I know you will soon be creating your masterpiece," Nita tells him with great confidence and is able to motivate him with her assurance. She winks at Mini and Aman catches her winking at the pillar next to her. He is surprised at Nita's reaction but does not make any comment. He speaks to her in a perplexed voice as his mind tries to process Nita's strange behaviour. "What exactly are you doing in this school? What course are you attending?" Aman asks Nita. "I am taking the personality development classes," Nita tells him as Aman looks at her surprised. "Personality development, do you really need such classes? I find you to be very determined, confident and a person with a pleasing personality. Wonder why you enrolled for this class," Aman says in disbelief.

Nita is surprised at Aman's remarks. "I am the nervous type, a weakling who is lacking total confidence,…I mean I was lacking total confidence till I joined the classes and have improved slightly in the last few days," Nita tries to explain to Aman who does not agree with her assessment of herself. "I don't think so. I find you very smart, cheerful, confident, assertive, social and graceful," Aman tells Nita. "Maybe you have joined the school to just admire my paintings," Aman remarks jokingly. Nita is elated to hear Aman talk about her with such admiration as it is the first time in her life that she has heard someone talk so well about her personality. Her confidence builds up as she asks Aman why he is in the school. "You too don't need to be here as you are an expert in your art, then what are you doing here, maybe you are here to admire my persona," Nita teases Aman. "I have been hopping from one job to the other but now I know that I want to take up painting as a profession and this is the reason that has brought me here for honing and perfecting my art skills and techniques," Aman explains his reason for joining the art classes to Nita. "That would be great, Aman. You will be an extremely successful and renowned artist, the most sought after, giving people autographs and selling each piece of your art for billions," Nita tries to predict Aman's future bringing a smile on his face. "Now you are pulling my leg," Aman tells Nita. Nita shakes her head and says, "No, I am not. I am very serious and I believe it. Just look at your work. It is just magnificent! It is beyond this world! You will be famous very soon." Aman smiles and tries to believe what Nita has just said.

Pam overhears a part of their conversation and comes running to join them with envy growing in her heart and colouring her thoughts. "Hi, did you say famous, who is going to be famous soon, Aman, you paint well but yes, famous, maybe," Pam does not believe Nita and gets jealous of Aman's work, her face turns red with anger and her eyes seem to be full of envy as she bites her lip and stomps her foot and turns towards the easel. She picks up a bottle of black colour and says bye to Aman and Nita. She turns around to leave and looks at the canvas and the rising sun which is screaming at Pam that Aman will be tasting success soon. In her fit of envy she splashes the black colour on the sun and walks out of the class as Aman and Nita stand petrified on witnessing her heinous deed. Aman's classmate

Deep witnesses this atrocious behaviour from Pam and stands speechless looking at Aman and Nita, who too are in a state of shock. It takes him a while before he returns to his senses and walks up to Aman and Nita and talks to them about the incident. The three of them stand their shocked and helpless with no words being said between them as words cannot describe the low deed and words cannot make good the loss made by her act. Aman's work has been totally ruined by her envy. "She is mad, no......she is so jealous that she has ruined your work," Nita says in her hoarse voice as she is almost in tears. "It is okay, don't cry, I will be able to fix this soon, don't worry," Aman tries to pacify Nita even though he is hurt and in pain. Nita cannot believe that jealousy can make a person stoop so low. Aman looks at his canvas and starts mixing some colours on the palette for retrieving the original charisma of the painting. Nita looks at him in admiration in spite of her pain at seeing the condition of the painting and asks, "You have so much patience, how come the incident did not arouse your anger?" Aman smiles at her and says, "You were almost in tears and would have cried if I had got angry so I had to keep my cool." Nita is again left in respect for Aman and his strong character. She tries her best to smile at him as she controls her tears and leaves for the day as Aman gets busy with his brush strokes to redo his painting and revive its magic. Deep is standing beside Aman in an attempt to support him in his hour of loss with his face showing signs of his sorrow and pain as he points to the canvas when Mr. Sharma returns from the Principal's office. "What happened Deep?" he questions Deep as he sees him pointing towards Aman's painting. Deep explains to him as he stammers in his anxiety and Aman completes his narration of the incident leaving Mr. Sharma in shock too. "I will take action against her. I will suspend her for a week," Mr. Sharma says to Aman and Deep. "It is okay sir, I do not think that will change her outlook," Aman says. "No, I must, she cannot get away with this," Mr. Sharma is adamant in taking action against Pam and goes to the Principal's office again to speak to her for initiating disciplinary action against Pam.

Nita is shocked at Pam's behaviour and is unable to believe that jealousy can take such an ugly shape that it has made a person lose her sanity and stoop so low to portray such a negative shade of her character. Pam had been unreasonable and gone out of control of her senses under the spell of envy. "Mini, why did Pam stoop so low today? How could she behave so negatively? Poor Aman, he must be so hurt. He will have to make the painting all over again. He had made a beautiful piece of art and Pam just ruined it out of jealousy. I just can't believe what I saw her do," Nita speaks to Mini with anger on Pam's behaviour, anguish on her own helplessness for not having taken any action and frustration for Aman who will have to make his painting all over again. Mini listens to Nita with patience and tries to calm her down. "Nita, Pam could not control her emotions and her behaviour reflected her lack of self-esteem and you can see her work, it is shabby and she knows at the bottom of her heart that she can never be as good as Aman but she is unable to accept this fact. Aman behaved in a matured fashion by keeping his cool and controlling his anger," Mini tells Nita. "Hope she realizes her mistake and apologizes to Aman," Nita says hopefully though she is dejected and wonders how one can get so jealous and behave irrationally. She is hurt and feels bad for Aman, a strange feeling, a sensation when you can feel the pain of someone else as your own, be one with another soul. "I really feel very sorry for Aman, hurts to see his painting wrecked by Pam, I am glad that Sharma Sir took action and suspended her for a week but will she learn from it is another question that remains to be answered," Nita continues in her sad voice as she looks at Mini for consolation with her heart yearning to be with Aman and be his support in her hour of need. Tears start to flow from her eyes and she is unable to understand what grieves her so much, Pam's devious actions, Aman's inaction or Aman's pain that must be immense though he tried his best to keep calm in the grave situation. She is hurt because Aman is hurting and she can feel his pain as her heart wrenches in misery and she cries for a long time with Mini by her side who is sad to see Nita in so much pain, a pain that comes from the feeling of oneness with another, a divine feeling called love!

Nita forgets to even watch her favourite show on television as she is grieving and hurt. Kaya and Shan are unable to understand the sudden change in their daughter's behaviour. "She had been so chirpy yesterday and now.....what could have happened to make her feel so low?" Kaya asks

Shan who is reading the newspaper. "Let her handle it herself. We should give her some time. Must be something at the school....you know how it is when you are in a class with students from different walks of life....we should give her space and watch for a day or two before we try and step in to help her out," Shan replies as Kaya nods at him knowing that Shan is right in his decision about Nita.

Chapter 10

"Mini, we asked Mom for six months and two weeks are already over, time just flies! I have made so many good friends at the school. I feel blessed to be in their company and Aman is the best of all friends that I have at the school. He is such an understanding and caring person. He understands me so well and I do not need to pretend when I am with him, I can be myself and not worry about anything when he is around," Nita talks to Mini as she prepares for a debate at the school. "He is almost like this room, …., a shade, so comforting that I can let my hair down and be myself when I am with him, he is such a good friend and a very good human being who is so genuine that I can trust him any time. He is really a very nice person who has never smirked or frowned at me or mocked anything that I do. He has never made me feel different like others do, in fact, I feel very confident and comfortable in his presence. He helps me be what I am and that is so important for me. And his work is so divine. He creates magic with his colours. I just cannot stop admiring his creations that have a soul and each one of them has an extraordinary theme which speaks of the depth of his thoughts and emotions. I find myself at peace when I am with him and that makes him so special. I cannot imagine my day at the school without him. His presence is like the most wonderful thing that has happened to me. Mini have you seen him? He is so different, just adorable and his nature sets him apart from everyone else. Is he not the best? The artist in him is so superior and yet he is so humble. I have never met such an accomplished person who is so modest and simple. I think it is his simplicity which makes him so lovable,….did I say lovable,….I think I meant his simplicity sets him apart and above the rest. I feel wrapped in his care when I am with him and that makes him so special," Nita thinks about Aman with peace reigning her heart and bliss on her joyful face. "Yes, he is definitely different and you seem to have taken a strong liking for him. He too seems to admire you each time we meet him," Mini tells Nita who is lost in Aman's thoughts. Aman has definitely changed her and brought a new ray of light and hope in her life.

Her thoughts get interrupted as her face twitches on getting a passing thought about Dani, a man whose behaviour is unpardonable, a very annoying person and a constant trouble maker. "Mini, that guy Dani is so evil and nasty. He lacks manners and is so wicked in his comments towards me. I wish he were not there in the class," Nita confides in Mini. "You should not let him control your behaviour and your emotions at all Nita, he is just insecure as his knowledge is mediocre and he does nothing to improve it but finds solace in ridiculing those who are better than him. I do not think you should give him any importance, he is just there in the class to while away his time, and has no intention of learning," Mini tries to make Nita understand. Nita feels better after having spoken to Mini and assures herself that she will not let Dani come in her way and she tries to think how she can counter his comments or change her behaviour that will help make him stop his pranks.

Nita meets Aman before her class begins the next morning as she wants to catch a glimpse of his latest work and also see if he has recovered from the shock of Pam's demeaning behaviour. Nita is relieved and happy to see Aman at ease and peace with himself making a new painting. "You are here early today," Aman tells Nita. "Just thought of coming over to see you before my class starts, ...just to see if you are okay," Nita tells Aman as she looks at him to make sure that he is feeling fine and recovered from the incident. "I am okay,......things are just okay, don't worry," Aman says with a reassurance in his voice that comforts Nita. Aman is extremely happy to see care in Nita's eyes that speaks of her concern for him which touches his heart and floods it with immense joy which reflects in his painting that turns out brighter than expected.

Aman finds Nita disturbed and tries to find the reason that upsets her. "It is Dani, an evil boy in the class who makes it a point to tease me and ridicule me so that I lose my confidence and make a fool of myself in front of the whole class," Nita tells Aman in a distressed and sad voice. Aman is hurt but does not let Nita know and tries his best to make her feel better. "You should not let him affect you in any way. Why do you react when he says anything? The best way to deal with him is not to react when he instigates you. Your indifference will kill him and his ego. Try it and you will feel better," Aman guides and motivates Nita. "Thanks Aman. I feel so much better after talking to you. I will do as you say and I am sure things will get better," Nita tells Aman with a little cheer in her voice. Aman is able to bring her smiles and cheerfulness back with his caring nature and their bond is growing stronger day by day as they have a better understanding of each other. Nita is happy to have him as her friend and mentor, someone she can always depend upon and look up to for guidance, a pillar of support, dependable in every situation and caring for her smallest need. She is confident of facing Dani with courage after speaking to Aman who has encouraged her to gather her strength and face every challenge in life. Dani is her latest challenge as his sole aim in life seems to be to discourage Nita. Nita has made up her mind to stand strong and not allow Dani to shake her confidence even by a whisker.

Chapter 11

Nita is asked to make a speech again and this does not leave her as nervous as it generally does as her confidence has been growing gradually and the day sees her well in control over her nervous self as she stands with a regal poise and walks to her seat like an Empress who is set to conquer the world and vanquish all her enemies. She gets busy jotting down some points in her diary and makes some notes for her speech and is soon ready to face the class. It is a moment that sees Nita stand up with great confidence but her face soon sees marks of distress as she feels a pull at her hand and Dani snatches her diary from her very discretely and whispers to her as she is walking away from her seat, "Let us see how you make the speech today, Ms. Nervous!" Dani teases Nita with a twisted smile on his face. Nita is taken unawares with Dani's sudden act making her very angry with Dani for his rude behaviour, a feeling of dejection at his childlike attitude, leaving her disturbed and upset shaking her confidence a little as she had made notes for her speech in the diary which is now in Dani's possession. Dani is confident that Nita will fumble and falter and make a laughing stock of herself and this has him rejoicing with a feeling of defeating her in the match of her life. Dani turns towards the class and winks at the students with an obnoxious smile on his beastly face that projects his hellish intentions. Simi and Ajay have noticed his devilish act and look at him in dismay and then at Nita fearing this to be a catastrophic situation which could leave their friend distraught. Nita is a little unsure of herself before she nods her head and blinks her eyes at Simi and Ajay in a comforting mode as she has made up her mind to manage the speech well and knows that she will not let Dani get away with his cheap tricks. She smiles at her friends and faces the class with courage as she stands in front of them with total calmness and peace prevailing on her gentle face in spite of the rush of panic flowing through her mind.

"Good morning friends! I had thought of a different topic to speak about this morning but something happened just as I walked up here and I find it important to speak about another topic of relevance today. It was a moment of enlightenment for me as I walked from my seat to take my place here in front of you, an enlightenment that struck me with the speed of lightning that left me wondering on the pettiness of our lives, its issues and its people as what matters in life are the values that we imbibe from our families and our teachers and the rest is trivia, yes, rest is trivia, immaterial and too petty to be even given a passing thought," Nita begins her extempore speech with total confidence. Nita looks at Dani and smiles, "Life has different designs for each one of us and it takes us time to understand our individual designs. Some of us are so insecure about ourselves that we vent our worries by ridiculing others. It is a waste of time to vent these worries which turn self-destructive as time passes by. We should channelize these worries into our strength to look for our potential and tap the latent energy that exists within each one of us. We are born with a purpose and it is our duty and responsibility to find that purpose and that can only happen when we know our true strengths. It is easy to let our stress and weaknesses take shapes of negative outbursts of energy but the real challenge and success lies in building our strengths which are there in each one of us waiting for us to light that spark, the spark that will make our strengths grow, glow and catapult us to a life of prosperity with inner peace and strength of character. I would like to end my short speech today with a small question for us to deliberate upon, and that question is that have we found our light and if yes, have we put it to the right use and if not, are we trying to find it for giving up is a sign of cowardice, the courageous keep fighting till the end. Thank you," Nita closes her speech with an assertive tone and takes her seat while Dani looks at her in frustration as his plans to make her nervous have failed miserably. Nita's stance and the confidence on her face speaks of her indifference to trivial issues and people like Dani who do not matter to her at all, she has surpassed all pettiness in life and risen much higher to a level where she would not be affected by anyone and anything. She does not even look at Dani as he does not matter in her life anymore, there is no need for her to get even with him as that is an act of the lesser souls who spend their time in cheap gossip and tricks trying to bring about the downfall of others, she has realized these to be the signs of below average minds while she has moved on to a superior level where great ideas are discussed and deployed which can help the world at large, she has moved on and ahead leaving the pettiness of Dani far behind where his existence makes no difference to her. The speech makes Mr. Kumar and the students clap loudly, a long applause, and Mr. Kumar appreciates Nita's speech. "That was very philosophical and relevant to our class as you are all here with a purpose and in the process of discovering your true strengths, very well said Nita, great job. The use of words, punctuations, expressions and exactness in delivering the words as well as the entire speech has been superlative. You are emerging as a good speaker and can take over as a leader soon," Mr. Kumar comments on Nita's speech with great pride in his eyes to see his student excelling with time. Nita is happy and Simi and Ajay make a face at Dani as a sign of having conquered the battle field, they see themselves as warriors with swords in their hands with their hats rotating on the tip of the swords symbolic of their victory at the end of the battle, cheering their army which presently is a one lady army of Nita. Dani is left gaping as his prank failed to have the effect he wanted, he has been deprived of making fun of Nita's nervousness and that makes his frustration grow wild so he walks out of the class in disgust. Nita feels sorry for Dani and his weakness to be overpowered by his whims but is confident about herself and that brings a smile of contentment and peace on her face, a symbol of the knowledge that says she cannot be controlled by anyone anymore, she is on her own, an independent lady who can face life and manage on her own, a feeling of success as she has achieved what she set out for when she entered through the gates of the Arts School. She has two more months to go before she finishes the classes and fulfills her promise to her parents.

"I have to let my parents know about my speech today. I am sure they will be delighted to know about my progress. And Mini will jump up with joy,..........Mini?......Gosh,....where is she?" Nita talks to herself with a feeling of fulfillment which suddenly turns into despair at the thought of Mini. She feels very strange to have forgotten Mini and stranger at the thought that she did not need Mini's encouragement at all today. She did not need to look around to find Mini or talk to Mini throughout the day as she wrote her speech or got up to speak and even when Dani snatched her diary from her. Nita is a little confused about the fact that she totally ignored Mini today so she wants to apologize to her but does not find her around. Simi and Ajay start talking to her about the next class and Nita forgets to talk to Mini. The day passes by smoothly and she returns home contented and at peace, walks to the living room to speak to her parents about the things she is learning at her school and her speech that she gave with confidence and she even joins them for dinner. Kaya is surprised that Nita did not run into her room but came and sat with them which is definitely a good sign confirming that Nita is opening up to the world and is ready to communicate with human beings in addition to her soft toys. She is happy to note the change in Nita, a positive and welcome change that leaves Kaya smiling and there are a few tears in her eyes, the tears of seeing her daughter coming out of her shell, the tears of happiness at her daughter's success in facing the challenges of life, the tears of joy to know her daughter is ready to face the world. She looks at Shan through her tears and sees him smiling at her. "Why do I see tears in your eyes? Things are looking up now and that should make you happy, don't want to see you crying when our daughter is changing for the better," Shan tells Kaya with a sense of pride in his voice. Kaya nods her head and smiles at Shan, a smile that speaks of her immense happiness and contentment on seeing her daughter progress through her life with a confidence that has gradually built up and paved the way for her to take on life's challenges. Nita is happy to see her parents speak about her. It is a day of great pride, happiness and peace for Ashiana today!

Chapter 12

———◆✕◆———

Aman paints a beautiful mask with its multiple reflections in the ripples of the ocean and gives every mask a different emotion, joy, anger, fear, grief, laughter, hatred, anxiety and curiosity. He wants to show case this painting as his masterpiece at the school exhibition which is generally held at the end of the session. He paints and repaints to gain perfection on his canvas with each mask narrating a different story with detailed expressions that are so clear that they seem to come alive on the canvas. He wants to give each mask a new colour with its shades radiating from the mask and merging with the colours of the next mask. He uses another canvas for practicing his brush strokes and to finalize the shades for the masks, the second canvas has a plethora of shades of blues, greens and yellows on it in brush strokes spanning its entire body in various directions. Nita comes to meet him in the afternoon and finds him in the campus lawn in front of his easel busy with his brush strokes that have an amazing fluid quality that makes them flow like a gentle unharnessed wave on his canvas with such perfection that she gapes at him stunned to see his marvellous work. She does not want to distract him so she waits patiently hoping for him to turn around and notice her but her wait seems to be endless as she stands there like a statue behind him and can feel herself waiting till eternity and as she cannot live without talking to him, she taps him very gently on his shoulder with the tip of her finger to bring him back to this world.

Aman is too busy to notice Nita standing behind him as he is totally engrossed in perfecting his painting for the exhibition. He is moving his brush across the cheeks of the mask with the expression of joy when he feels a gentle tap on his shoulder, very gentle, a caress so soft, softer than that of a feather that has touched his soul as he turns around to see Nita who stands there like an angel bringing him a long needed respite from the drudgery of the world to emancipate him from his loneliness, setting him and his heart free, bringing a new meaning to his life making it seem worthy of living and abundantly joyous. He stands mesmerized in admiration of the beautiful lady who looks like God's own painting and her soft touch has a divine charm to persuade his heartstrings to feel an emotion that he has never experienced before, plucking them into a soft tune that makes him freeze in the moment as the world around him has come to a standstill to hold time at this glorious enchanting moment. Nita looks at him in amazement as she has never noticed his handsome face before, a face that is a painting so captivating that she cannot take her eyes off him, his dark brown eyes give his face a definition and he is lost in her beauty that is so charismatic that it sways his heart and mind away into a far off land of a dreamy delusion where he cannot see anything apart from her pretty face and hear nothing apart from her melodious voice and they both wish for this dream to be everlasting. Nita finds it impossible to take her eyes off him and move them to the canvas but she tries her best to do so and that brings Aman out of his meditation too and they try to look away from each other but their eyes refuse to obey their minds and their hearts bring them back to adore each other as there is a silent communication of their eyes that takes them to their souls that talk without any words being spoken or heard. Nita again tries to look away and moves to the canvas reluctantly and breaks the silence that has kept their souls in unison. "Hi, ..., aa,....... ah,......this canvas looks so beautiful Aman...., very beautiful," Nita remarks as she looks at the second canvas but her eyes are trying to steal a look of Aman from their corner as her eyelashes try to remain arched to let them see him to her heart's content as her eyes know they are in love but her mind and heart are yet to learn and perceive this supreme feeling that is magnificent and divine. Aman fidgets as he is brought back abruptly from his beautiful dream and looks around and sees Nita staring at his second canvas wonderstruck while his mind is reliving the gentle tap that has redefined his world with a deluge of emotions that he is unable to judge or comprehend. "Oh,.....,ya,.....this one, this is my rough canvas, I,.....use this for practicing my brush strokes and finalizing the shades," Aman tells Nita with a smile. Nita looks askance at him and then at the painting and takes a deep breath before she comments on the painting though her heart and mind are lost in interpreting the look on Aman's face that appeared from the tap on his shoulder while Aman is trying to decipher his feelings that are strange and new and his reactions to Nita's tap on his shoulder that brought life into his meaningless world. "Your rough work is so mesmerizing, I just cannot believe that this is just a rough sketch, it is a masterpiece in itself. I wonder what your real masterpiece would be like, I just can't wait to see it Aman," Nita says in her excitement and in her nervousness as she tries to cope with her new found feelings that she has no control over and neither can she surmise. Aman shows her the mask painting with great pride in anticipation of getting wonderful comments for it. Nita is wonderstruck and her eyes move through each point of the painting as she admires Aman's work though her mind is in a confused state. "Your painting speaks through its colours and leaves me in a trance as I feel so dreamy adoring each dot of your creativity. It is so divine, each mask has a story to narrate, I just love it Aman," Nita looks at Aman with awe and admiration at the superiority of his creativity which has a magical spark that makes him stand much above the rest. Aman swells up with pride and joy as Nita's words make him feel like a big achiever. "Thanks Nita, you make me feel so complete. Your appreciation matters a lot to me and your words are like a downpour in a parched desert. I have been struggling to make something that would win adulation from viewers and your words are the biggest award that I can ever win," Aman says to Nita with a beautiful smile that brings stars in his dark brown eyes and makes her heart flutter with a new feeling that Nita has never felt before, a feeling so precious that it makes her feel complete, a wonderful emotion that has her totally entwined in its beautiful grip and control. Nita cannot take her eyes off Aman as he gets busy with his painting. Nita realizes that she is in love with Aman, love..., a feeling so gentle and yet so strong, the sense of merging of two souls into one that makes her eyes look dreamy and mystical. She cannot help but smile all through the day. Love has struck and brought Nita all the joy in the world, a feeling of gratification that makes her thank God for making her fall in love, a beautiful gift that is bestowed only on the blessed ones, a blessing that is supreme, a song that is complete, a painting drawn by God Himself. Love has brought a constant smile on Nita's face that spreads to her eyes which are twinkling with the dreams of Aman as her world is drenched with love that keeps her happy and lost in her dreamland where there is the highest contentment of having a feeling growing within you that makes you feel so complete, a waterfall that floods her world with jubilation and leaves her detached from the worries of the world. She has found strength and courage in love that has enhanced her confidence to confront anything in the world with ease, a feeling that lends power to her as nothing else matters to her in the world now. She misses Aman and her eyes keeps looking for him, making her run to meet him and admire his work making her create excuses for going to Aman's class and spend hours with him after her class. Her presence helps Aman perfect his work with greater dedication and enthusiasm to bring out the best of his potentials and capabilities. His art sees stupendous growth leaving him amazed at himself and such is the power of love that can make two souls bond into perfection and motivate each other to augment their strength and competence to outperform in their fields with the support of their love. His paintings have a rare quality which is being nurtured by love to infuse them with the colour of love that has enhanced their magic to a level of divinity. Nita's performance at her class has grown at different scales over the weeks with a slow and gradual improvement in the beginning to an exponential level after meeting Aman who has been instrumental in shaping her personality into a magnetic and charismatic abundance of confidence that exudes in every stance she takes.

Chapter 13

———◆◆◆———

Mr. Sharma gives Aman an assignment to work on a live subject and Aman chooses his favourite bench at the Maxing Garden, the bench he calls his 'thinking bench', apt for this project. "Choose a live scene and paint it," Mr. Sharma tells Aman. Aman sets off to the Maxing Garden and sets his easel in front of the bench and begins to sketch the bench with the mountains in the backdrop giving the sky a touch of the sun at dusk with dark green trees at a distance and his hands invariably paint a lady sitting on the bench as he imagines Nita sitting on the bench with her hair flowing in the breeze and covering her face, like an angel hiding her pretty face from the world. He suddenly realizes that Nita has taken the centre stage of his life as he can only think about her.

Nita has to meet Aman after her class and rushes to his wing. She is distressed on not seeing him there making her heart grow restless as her eyes keep looking for him all around the campus. She calls him on his mobile but it is not reachable adding to her growing restlessness, her heart is twitching and she feels it to be falling into a vacuum and it hurts her.

Aman draws her right hand attempting to hold her hair from covering her face, a beautiful hand with long and pretty fingers that seem to be fighting the force of the breeze with their gentle grip trying to grasp her hair with care. Aman is admiring the painting of Nita that he has just created and it adds to his restlessness as he misses her more on seeing the painting.

Nita learns that Aman has been given an outdoor assignment and he will not be there for the next two days which makes her feel miserable as she misses him, a feeling that a part of her has distanced from her, a feeling of being lost in the wide world, a heaviness of the heart that tears it apart as she thinks about him.

Aman closes his eyes and sees Nita and her hands, her fingers and the little diamond ring on her finger and he paints the ring with great fondness which completes his painting.

Nita tries to find out where Aman has gone and she asks Simi to ask Mr. Sharma in her desperation to find him making Simi wonder why she is in such despair. "Simi, can you please check and let me know where Aman is? I am sure Sharma Sir would know," Nita urges Simi to find Aman's whereabouts and soon learns he is at Maxing Garden.

Aman steps back to look at the painting and cannot take his eyes off Nita sitting on his bench, he keeps admiring her and a little later sees Nita turning her face towards him and smiling at him. He smiles back and knows his painting is ready, he has unknowingly brought Nita permanently in his life as he cannot paint anything apart from her and she has even taken over his 'thinking bench'.

"Here you are and I have been looking all around the world for you," Nita says in her misery as she walks up to Aman. Aman looks at her in total shock and awe thinking he must be dreaming and looks around to see if Nita has walked out of the canvas but finds her sitting on the bench so he turns around and sees Nita standing there with her hair flying in the breeze trying to cover her eyes and he notices a tear drop in her eye. "Are you crying? Why are you crying? And what are you doing here? How did you know that I am here today?" Aman asks her as she is standing there baffled trying to come to her senses, her heart is still twitching and she wants to capture his image in her eyes and does not want to look away for the fear of losing sight of him again. She seems to have found her breath and life on seeing Aman, feeling like a fish that has been put back into the water to revive it as she feels life returning into her limbs, her words are just short of a mumble and her heart is beating too fast on seeing him. Aman is amazed shocked and keeps staring at her. Nita finally manages to talk, "I found out you are here,……..was looking for you all around the campus, ……….I went mad searching for you,……you should have at least informed me that you are here, …..I was trying your phone,…why do you carry a phone that does not work,…….do you know how the last three hours have been for me,……..do you have any idea,……do you?"

Aman is looking at her spellbound, his heartbeat is very different and his mind is unable to understand what is happening to him and to Nita, he is mesmerized by her beauty and confused by her comments and bewildered at himself as he is very excited and elated to see her there, like a dream come true, his painting has come alive and his heart is tasting the aroma of love which leaves him astounded and speechless as he stands there adoring Nita. Nita is frustrated at Aman's indifference to her questions but decides not to say anything to him as she does not want to hurt him, he has become so important in her life that his feelings have gained the top importance for her. She notices the easel and looks at the painting and starts walking towards it in a trance of magnetism which pulls her towards the canvas, her eyes admiring the painting and her heart thinking about Aman. She keeps staring at the bench and at the girl sitting on the bench as Aman waits eagerly for her comments and appreciation. His eyes are restless as they attempt their best to behold her beauty and his heart is feeling a twitch and a pull and his mind lost in her beautiful thoughts but he manages to ask her views about the painting. The breeze blows again and Nita holds her hair from falling on her face as she is admiring the painting and she realizes that what she is seeing on the canvas is a mirror image of the present situation as she clasps her hair and moves them behind her ear. She looks at the ring in the painting and turns her hand to look at her ring, she knows it is her, Aman has painted her, a feeling of joy grips her as she looks at Aman with stars in her eyes. Aman glances at her and smiles and is at a loss of words and there does not seem to be a need for words when they are with each other. "I am sorry,.........it is my mistake,.... I should have told you that I will be here, but I am glad that you are here to see my work. Do you like it?" Aman asks Nita. Nita is under a spell, the spell of love and takes time to recover before she can respond to Aman's question, "I love it, it is very beautiful, I feel I am a part of the painting, the ring is like mine, ... just love the way this bench is holding a life while the sun is setting and the mountains and trees are bidding goodbye to the day." Aman loves her description of his work which is so articulate that makes him feel proud of his work. "Yes, you are right, it is you on the bench, I drew my bench, ...I call it my bench as this is the bench I like to while away my time on,.........

then I drew the mountains, the skies and the trees but my painting was incomplete without you so I painted you on the bench and I like the way the breeze blows your hair and covers your face so I added that and then I still felt something was missing in your hand so I painted your ring on it," Aman tells Nita as she looks at him with all her love on hearing that his painting was incomplete without her, the thought that he was thinking about her makes her overjoyed, a feeling of total peace, attainment of the highest level of happiness and completeness on completing someone's life and especially when that someone is the most special person of your life. The day is one of the most beautiful days in both Nita and Aman's lives as they sit on Aman's 'thinking bench' and talk till late evening, trying to get to know each other and spending some more time together.

Chapter 14

---◆◆◆◆◆---

It is another day at the school and Nita has to join a group discussion on finding solutions for increasing the availability of food to feed the ever growing population of the world. She has Simi, Ajay, Raja and Deepak in her group. The team nominates Nita as the leader for their group. There are two more groups of five students each. The three groups have been given an hour to discuss the topic within their group and present their views to the rest of the teams. There is a healthy and meaningful discussion by the students of her group as she manages to control the flow of thoughts and the focus on the topic of discussion though her mind keeps running to Aman. She is multi-tasking as her heart is with Aman and a part of her mind is with the group and the balance grey cells are lost in Aman's thoughts. Nita's life has suddenly become very complex with the need to split her focus and attention between Aman and the rest of the world. Her family has unexpectedly taken a back seat as Aman has emerged as the centre of attraction of her life by sweeping her off her feet literally as she has tripped a number of times while running from her classroom to his in a hurry to be with him. Mr. Kumar asks the leaders to summarize the discussion and present it to the class. Nita starts her presentation with full confidence even though her mind is with Aman, she tries her best to focus on her presentation and begs her mind to pause her thoughts for a little while and help her complete the speech.

"Good Morning friends and Kumar Sir, it is a great morning today and we have had the opportunity to discuss a subject which is of prime importance in the world today, the availability of food versus the growth in population and how we can make food available for the growing population of the world. Simi, Ajay, Raja, Deepak and I have just tried to dwell on the subject and each one of us has come up with some solutions that can be implemented to counter the problem and make food available for the growing population of the world. We have to equip ourselves to have food for the generations to come and it is our responsibility as the youth of our nation to create awareness about the problem at hand and bring about the change by raising the issue to the government and the designated authorities to take action. We are sure that government must have deliberated on this subject and implemented solutions too but here we have come up with our recommendations based on our discussion on the subject. I will summarize the group's thoughts which we feel can help in increasing the availability of food for the growing population of the world. First and foremost there is a need to curtail wastage of food as a measure to save what is already available with us. There is wastage of crop due to lack of storage facilities and there is wastage of food if cooked in excess. We need to bring about awareness and develop methods to control these wastages. Secondly, government can give subsidy on seeds and agricultural equipment to help the poor farmers in growing crops as many farmers are unable to afford seeds, manure and equipment and hence there is a need to help them and subsidizing these can help the farmers to a large extent. Thirdly, we need to encourage the young farmers to take up full scale farming as the youth is moving to bigger towns and cities for better prospects leaving farming in the hands of a limited number of people, we need to increase the hands that till the land if we need more crop. Fourthly, the farmers need to get incentives and higher profits for the crops grown by them and that can be made possible by reducing the middlemen to give the farmers their rightful dues and motivate them to grow more crops. Fifth point that we came up with is that there is a need to increase job opportunities for people to be able to buy food as food may go waste if it is available but there are no buyers for it. This is the crux of our discussion today. Thank you friends, you may give us your suggestions too. I will now ask my team members to come up here one by one and take you through each solution in detail." Simi, Ajay, Raja and Deepak take the stage one by one and speak on the solutions in detail as Nita stands with them with her heart and mind lost in Aman's thoughts.

There is a thunderous applause from Mr. Kumar and the students that makes Nita and her group feel delighted, a sense of accomplishment from having got a desirable response on the efforts made by them, a great achievement. Nita is happy but her mind is still thinking about Aman, she wants the class to be over soon and free her from its clutches to make her rush to Aman. Mr. Kumar appreciates the group and their thought process and congratulates Nita for having emerged as a great speaker. Nita is thankful to Mr. Kumar and thanks her group members though her mind is elsewhere, she is seeing Aman and his canvas, his hands move gently with the brush strokes and his handsome eyes are forever fixed on his canvas, he is her Prince Charming who has overpowered her mind and heart and she cannot think of anything else but Aman. She cannot wait for the next two presentations to get over so that she can run to Aman's class and be there with him to admire him till he tells her to go home though she would want to be there forever with him. The next two presentations are also very good but Nita has cut off her hearing ability to avoid listening to the class as she wants to hear her heartbeat that is moving at the speed of a jet and she is again drifting into Aman's thoughts. Nita is baffled as time does not seem to move, tying Nita down to her seat while her heart is missing Aman and her mind is floating through the skies to be with Aman, a feeling of divinity as she can hear him speak, it is a soul speaking to the other, a telepathy that bonds two hearts in spite of the physical distances that separate them, a tearing of the heart to be away from him that is causing her so much pain that she cannot bear it anymore and that brings her back to the class and she hears someone talking to her. "Nita, where are you lost? We need to leave now. Let us go," Simi tells her as Nita tries to wake up from her dream with love sparkling through her beautiful dark brown eyes. She nods her head and says, "Let us go check Aman's new painting. I had promised him that we will be there in the afternoon today. Ajay, do you want to come along too?" Ajay nods and they set off for Aman's class.

Nita comes to Aman's class with Simi and Ajay to see his latest creation and to meet him as his presence is the elixir of her life. Aman always looks forward to Nita's visit as she is full of admiration for his work but now he is only waiting to meet her, see her and talk to her. She goes through his paintings thoroughly and appraises them with the expertise of a mature artist with an eye for detail. She is the best fan of his work; a fan who goes through every stroke of his brush and appreciates each shade of colour used by him in his art and even criticizes his work whenever it is not meeting her expectations. Aman has a new theme for his painting which makes his work look very different from the rest of his paintings, a very different style and a new and unique use of colours. He has the panoramic view of a city on display on his easel which catches Nita's attention and she looks at each building and their windows with wonder. She loves the roads and the streetlights painted on the canvas which have a life infused in them. "These look so real Aman I almost feel I am walking on this road with buildings flanking me on both sides. I can feel the streetlights blinding me as I walk through the street. I seem to find myself as a part of this painting. The lights are glowing like they are actually there for real and I cannot believe that this is a painting. I just love this work," Nita speaks in admiration of Aman's work while Ajay's eyes are glowing in admiration of Nita as he sees her talk to Aman.

Aman notices Ajay staring at Nita and feels very uncomfortable, a feeling which is very new for Aman, a strange tearing of the heart and a twitch that makes him feel jealous of Ajay as he suddenly feels very possessive of Nita and this arouses anger in him. He snaps at Nita, "It is okay Nita, no big deal, I don't think this painting is very good, I am busy and do not want to be disturbed, you can come back later," Aman speaks to Nita in a very harsh tone leaving Nita gaping at him in utter confusion and a state of shock. "What is wrong with him? Why is he behaving like this?" Nita thinks to herself and feels very hurt. She just walks out of the room with Simi and Ajay following her as her eyes are moist as they look at Aman with a stream of love flowing through them with her tears. Aman is very hurt, not hurt just because of seeing Ajay adore Nita but hurt by hurting Nita with his rudeness and he is shocked on hurting the person he cherishes the most in this world. He is finding it difficult to pardon himself for his behaviour. "Why did I speak to Nita like that? It was very wrong. I hurt her. I was hurting and I just took off my anger on Nita. I should not have ….," Aman keeps thinking about Nita and tears his painting in his frustration, a frustration that is not just anger but the pain of love, he realizes he loves Nita and he was not able to see Ajay admire her as he loves her, he has grown possessive of her making him react the way he did. He cannot forget the tears in her eyes and the pain on her pretty face which has been caused by him and that is hurting him more and more. This pain is the pain of love as he can feel her pain and his heart cries for her, a pain that he has never felt before, his heart is wrenching and all he can see is Nita, his canvas looks like Nita and his brush seems to be in Nita's hands as she tries to paint something on his canvas. Aman is seeing Nita all around him and he notices her beautiful dark brown eyes that have sparkles in them, a glow on her face that he has never seen before, her hair that fall on her cheeks which have started to make his heart miss a beat, her smile that has never been so bewitching that it takes his breath away, he is lost in her thoughts and cannot break away from them, a feeling so beautiful yet painful, a new feeling that has taken charge of his faculties, a sensation that makes his heart flutter, a breeze of fresh air that sings a melodious song and there is no other sound that he can hear and he cannot feel the presence of anyone else around him, a new and strange emotion that is overwhelming, a divine sense of his soul merging with hers, love that is making him smile and bringing stars in his eyes and a dreamy mythical magic that is pulling the strings of his heart to conjure a song for his soul, the world has suddenly changed into a mystical ocean with Nita as the only inhabitant apart from him, love which is growing to immerse him in it. "I,.......I have hurt her, I need to apologize to her, ...because I love her,........., yes I do, this is the best feeling that I ever had, I feel totally captivated by her," Aman talks to himself and dials her number only to learn that her mobile is switched off. He panics and runs to the other wing of the building to look for Nita, his eyes can see her all around but still cannot find her bringing fear of the unknown, a fear that she may not have run away and left him all alone, a fear of losing her forever, a fear of having hurt her beyond repair. Nita is not in her class and that worries Aman, he is in a state of shock and too afraid to admit that his eyes might let loose some tears as the thought of losing her is the most painful one which rips his heart apart and his mind is clouded with the worst thoughts of the world trying to separate him from Nita. He goes around the campus in search of Nita like a sheep that has gone too far from the herd and is unable to return home, he is so lost, lost in search of his love, terrified at the very thought of losing his love till he reaches the end of the campus and there is a ray of light that brings a faint smile on his tired face. He sees a beautiful soul sitting under a tree, a soul that is his own, he looks at Nita with a deluge of love pouring from his eyes drenching the world with the cascade of love flowing from his heart and he walks towards her as though he is walking in his dream. "She looks pretty even when she is sad," Aman thinks to himself as he walks up to Nita, his love, his life, his heart and his soul, the very meaning of his life.

"Nita, ….I am sorry, Nita………, I should not have behaved the way I did, I am really sorry," Aman says to Nita as she looks at him with sorrow painted all across her face. "I know I hurt you, ….., I tore the painting that made me hurt you, Nita," Aman tries to console Nita but leaves her shocked instead. "Tore the painting, ……….but why? Why did you do that Aman? It was such a beautiful painting," Nita says in her disbelief, she tries not to believe him but is pained to see the truth in his eyes. "I had to, it made me hurt your feelings, I did not mean to talk the way I did, I do not know what got over me, ……..it was Ajay,…….. the way he looked at you, …….it made me envious and it hurt me, I was in pain and anger and I just said whatever came to my mind, I am sorry, I know I was wrong, I was angry with Ajay but I shouted at you instead, I just could not bear to see him look at you like that, ………I cannot,………I ………I never will,……because I love you Nita,…..nobody has the right to look at you because you are mine,……no one but I can look at you," Aman tells Nita as Nita looks at him in surprise and there is a feeling of contentment as she knows Aman loves her. Life has suddenly become so beautiful and there is happiness all around, the world is filled with love, their love, she could not be happier, her heart is filled with all the joys of the world and her soul is drenched in love as she looks at Aman with stars adorning her pretty eyes and her face beaming with love. "You don't have to worry Aman, because I love you too," Nita tells Aman, the world seems to come to a halt, time stops at that very moment to bless them and congratulate them with the chimes of the heavens breaking into a song to bestow its gifts on Aman and Nita. The smiles on Aman and Nita's faces are stories of happiness that are painted on their hearts and souls which define love in its truest form, their souls have found the heavenly colours of their hearts which have extreme joy filled in their poetic shades making their hearts flap their wings and fly into the heavenly skies, Cupid has struck his arrow and is smiling at them from the heavens of the angels as these angles in love flow with the magic of the moment into a world of beauty, the skies are filled with the confetti of love sparkles and the two souls have learnt the oneness of love with their souls merging into one with a bond of togetherness, a bond forever and their life blooms with love.

Nita tries to say something to Aman but a voice interrupts her. "Oh, here you are and I have been looking all around the campus for you," Simi calls out to Nita. Nita and Aman are woken up from their trance. Nita looks at Simi and says, "Oh, ..., well,......I, ...oh, Aman was telling me about his new painting and I find it to be the best of all his works". She looks at Aman and sees love and admiration in his eyes which puts her in a trance again. "Where is it?" asks Simi. "What?" asks Nita in a dreamy stance as she is still staring at Aman with love pouring from her eyes. "The painting?" asks Simi. Aman tries to help Nita in answering Simi's question though he is still staring at Nita. "I have put my soul into this painting Simi," Aman smiles and looks at Simi and then back at Nita. "My new painting is drawn from the depths of my heart and soul," Aman winks at Nita and smiles. Nita smiles and looks at Simi, "Yes, it is really drawn from the depths of his heart and soul and is really very beautiful as it speaks volumes of his feelings....," Nita adds on as she is staring at Aman. Simi looks at both of them and finds them to be behaving strangely but keeps her feelings to herself. "Okay, I will see it soon but Nita can we leave now," Simi asks Nita. "Yes, you must go now," Aman tells Nita with his eyes glued to her face. Nita reluctantly says bye to him and leaves with Simi leaving a part of her with him as he sighs for he cannot bear to see her leave and she keeps turning around to get a glimpse of him as she too does not want to leave him, love is bonding their souls into one! Simi feels Nita and Aman are trying to hide something from her but cannot pin point at what it can be.

Chapter 15

—————◆◆◆—————

It is a day when Aman feels so lost that he has worked on his painting several times, unable to relate to what he has painted as it does not touch his heart, his painting lacks life and that makes him frustrated with his work. "There is something missing from this canvas," Aman tells Nita in his distressful voice. Nita can feel his anguish and dismay and is pained by it unable to see him stressed and torn. She looks at his painting closely and tries to help him, there is definitely something different about this painting as it lacks the life that Aman's creations generally have but she cannot say it directly to Aman as she fears hurting him with her opinion about his work. She smiles at Aman and says, "Why don't you paint me? Or anything that reminds you of me." Aman hugs her in his excitement and thanks her for the idea, sure he will paint her, he likes to paint her, the Maxing Garden painting also had Nita in it and looked like a masterpiece. "I will paint something that symbolizes your importance in my life," Aman declares to Nita and gets back to his canvas. Nita looks at him with great adulation and feels happy for him as she has tried to contain his tension and also helped him resume focus on his work. She leaves him alone with his work and returns to her class with his thoughts in her heart that keep her engaged in her dreamland while Mr. Kumar takes them through the lesson for the day.

Aman spends several hours on the canvas and calls Nita for her comments and waits for her to come running to meet him. He waits for ten minutes but grows restless and finds it difficult to wait for her so he walks to her class and finds her with Simi. "Hey Simi. Hi Nita, I wanted to show you guys something," Aman tells them. He takes them with him to his canvas taking long strides in his excitement as he cannot wait for Nita to admire his painting and give her awesome reviews on his creation.

Nita is left awestruck as she sees the beautiful sunrise and a rainbow and some clouds on the side. "This is the most important thing in my life, a sunrise that has brought light into my dull life and my pretty rainbow that has filled my life with all the colours of happiness and joy. This is the love of my life," Aman tells them as his eyes meet Nita's and she smiles, a smile that says she knows and understands what he is talking about, a smile that acknowledges her love for him and his love for her. She knows her importance in his life and that makes her feel on top of the world, Aman has made her the sunshine and the rainbow of his life, the extreme sense of being alive, being happy and being in the glory of the brightness of the sun. Aman and Nita have always been instrumental in helping each other to come out of their shadows into the light of life with the ability and strength to face the world and its challenges. Nita has grown confident and Aman is finding ways to deal with his failures and together they have been able to support each other to walk through the bad patches on their life's path. "I have to go home now, are you coming with me Nita," Simi asks Nita. "I will take some time. Why don't you go ahead, I will ask Aman to drop me," Nita tells Simi. "Okay, bye Nita, bye Aman," Simi says bye to them and leaves. "Bye Simi," Nita and Aman say to Simi in chorus.

Nita thanks Aman for making the painting and says, "Aman, I always feel that the man and woman you drew with their shadows, the ones walking along the beach, ...I think that's us, you know, the two of us walking together with the tests of life, trying to come out of our shadows with each other's support." Aman is wonderstruck as he looks at Nita and says," Yes, I also feel the same way. Strange that we think alike about everything in life, ...like two halves of the same soul. I have always believed that painting to be the story of our lives Nita and you have summed it up so well." Aman is admiring Nita as she adores his latest canvas sensing her joy that fills her heart on seeing his painting and the pride that she takes in his work. Life has tied Nita and Aman into a strong bond that they are nurturing with their affection and their love is growing stronger with time, a bond of a lifetime, a lifetime of love.

Life has become beautiful for Aman and Nita as they walk together coming out of their shadows to walk into the brightness of the golden sunshine, hand in hand, supporting, motivating and admiring each other and everything else in their lives has taken a backseat. Aman has got totally engrossed in his painting classes for perfecting his art skills but his mind and heart are forever lost in Nita's thoughts leaving very less time for his parents who are busy with their profession but not too busy to notice the change in their son, a change that has brought a determined, and focussed man who has found meaning and purpose in his life, a change that they had been wishing to see for years is blossoming in their home now bringing cheer in their dull life. Nita too has got focussed on her class and her thoughts are always filled with Aman leaving her no time for her parents and she does not even remember to speak to Mini, her best friend of all times, she is no more the timid girl who once lived in Ashiana but a person to reckon with, a person whose confident spirits are ready to face any challenge that life may hurl at her at any moment and with any velocity! Her parents are brimming with happiness to see the sea change in her attitude towards life and the confidence that is exuding from her new found personality. Love has graced these two souls with heavenly bliss!

Chapter 16

Nita picks up her books from the table and sees her pink teddy bear lying on her chair. "This one is the cutest and the softest," Nita says as she cuddles the teddy. "This is Mini's favourite toy,...............Mini?.............. strange I have not seen her for so many days now,.........it is stranger that I have not even spoken to her for a long time? Very strange, ... and where is she,.....Mini,......Mini where are you?" Nita suddenly remembers Mini and is extremely surprised and puzzled by her absence and from the strange revelation that her life has carried on for some weeks without Mini's existence, Mini who has been her only support and her best friend who helped her at every step of her life, but strangely she has not needed her motivation in recent weeks. "How can she just disappear? How could I carry on with my life without her?" Nita is buried in a flurry of questions and doubts with Mini's disappearance which has left her bewildered at the feasibility of her life without Mini. Nita starts looking around her room and terrace in search of Mini. "I am sure Mini is mad at me as I have not spoken to her, I need to find her and apologize to her for ignoring her. She must be hiding away in her anger," Nita talks to herself as she is trying to find Mini.

Kaya comes to Nita's room to speak to her and is surprised to find her talking to herself again, a shocking scene as Nita had stopped talking to her toys and to herself but now she is again repeating her silly habits. Kaya had been relieved to see Nita come out of her childhood habits but she is unhappy to see her reverting to her old self. Kaya cannot hide her anxiety and lashes out at Nita with her harsh words. "So Miss Nita, may I ask you, when are you going to stop your pretend games and grow up? You have had enough of pretending. It is high time you stopped talking to yourself. There are no friends around you. Your toys are not your friends.

Do you understand, they are not your friends! Do not give them names and characters that are larger than life. Snap out of your dreams and step into the real world, my daughter," Kaya tries to make Nita realize that Mini is non-existent. Nita looks at Kaya in dismay as though her favourite toy has been brutally snatched away from her hands leaving her alone under the open sky with the sun shining in its brightest and hottest avatar fuming in anger at her with its wrath. There are tears in her eyes as she looks at her mother for support, love and affection. "Mini does exist, she is right here," Nita tells Kaya in a convincing tone. "She is not here," asserts Kaya, "Look around you and you will not find her here. I am to be blamed for this situation Nita. I was too busy with my business and did not have much time for you Nita and you tried to find comfort in your toys and started talking to them, you gave them a larger than life character as you wanted their support. I feel sorry for having given you very little time which made you resort to a state of confinement in this room where you hide from the world. I should have been there for you when you needed me to boost your morale but I was travelling most of the time. I knew you were at peace with the toys and let you continue with your imaginary world but Mini is not there Nita and we have to confront this reality soon. Please come back to reality Nita, please…..you will have to walk out of your imaginary world as there is a real world that exists outside and you will have to face it soon." Nita looks around and does not see Mini in her chair. She is perplexed and again runs to the terrace to look for her but returns in dismay on not finding her anywhere. "Nita, Mini exists in your imagination, she is your inner voice, your alter ego, she is your superior self," Kaya tries to make Nita understand.

Nita looks at Kaya and turns to Mini's chair and walks around the room. She tries to recall the last time she saw Mini and is sadly not able to, she does not even remember the last time she spoke to her and that leaves her even more baffled. "Mini, where have you disappeared? Mini, Mini, ….," Nita runs around in a desperate search of Mini with her heart in her mouth and her forehead lines with creases from her worries and a tension that cannot be explained in words. Kaya shakes her head in disbelief and is worried with the thought that Mini's absence will make Nita restless and can have a negative effect on her life but in some hidden corner of her heart there is a hint of optimism that she wants to hold on to as it makes her believe that this incident could help Nita emerge as a stronger and confident person who does not need imaginary people to support her in leading her life. Kaya tries to calm her down and reason with her with logic. Nita is lost and confused as she is unable to understand why Mini has left her so abruptly like a sudden unexpected cloudburst on a sunny afternoon. She is not able to understand her mother's reasoning and she walks out of the room in a dizzy state of mind as she feels she has lost her best friend. As she walks out of the room she notices her reflection in the mirror in the corridor and stops to look at herself. She smiles as she sees Mini's reflection in the mirror and turns around to surprise her but Mini is nowhere around which leaves her puzzled. She looks back at the mirror and again sees Mini's reflection, Mini is smiling at her and Nita feels an outburst of happiness and peace reigning her world. Nita looks at the mirror with intrigue as she cannot see herself but it is Mini's reflection alone which leaves Nita aghast. She moves her hand across the mirror to wipe out Mini's reflection but is not able to and again turns around in an attempt to catch Mini standing behind her but alas, Mini is not there. She looks back at the mirror to see Mini standing there like a dream that is slowly fading away and Nita is able to see herself and Mini who seems to have merged with her. Nita notices for the first time that Mini looks exactly like her, like a twin sister. She stands there for long looking at herself trying to understand who she is and Mini seems to be a part of her whom she can relate to now with extreme clarity. Her mother was right and Mini was her brightness, her alter ego, the colour of her soul that defined her true and best potential, she was indeed a part of Nita. Mini had not disappeared but she had proved that she existed within Nita who perceived Mini to be a friend as she was the latent energy of her soul which remained unexplored till Nita grew aware of it and worked towards discovering and refining it. Mini was not required to exist as a separate entity in Nita's life now as Nita had emerged as Mini by empowering herself with her best potential and she had gained the confidence that she was lacking all this time. Nita is now a person of great confidence with a magnetic charm and pleasing personality and she smiles as she bids farewell to Mini through the mirror and thanks her mother for helping her see the reality and face it. Nita is on her own, a renewed soul with utmost confidence to face the world and its varied challenges. Nita no longer needs the support of an imaginary world as her inner confidence has flowered and grown to define her new radiant personality. She remembers her mother's words and goes back to her, she needs to speak to her and let her know how much she has helped her. "Mom, you were right, Mini does not exist as a person but as me, I am Mini and Mini is me. Thank you Mom for helping me see and face this reality and identify with myself, I do not want you to feel guilty about not giving me enough time. You were always there when I needed you Mom, you are the best Mom in the world," Nita says as she hugs her mother. Kaya and Nita have tears in their eyes as they confide in each other their innermost feelings and share a bond of love and understanding. The mother and daughter bond seems to strengthen as they embrace each other, an embrace that talks of their love for each other, their growing bond of friendship and the growing level of understanding between them. "Have I missed something?" Shan asks them as he enters Nita's room and sees his wife and daughter in tears hugging each other. "I have been looking all around for you. So what is this mother and daughter duo up to?" Shan asks them jokingly. Nita winks at Kaya and says, "Dad, we were having a special time together, you can join us too." Shan raises his eyebrow questioningly and says," I don't think so, there seems to be something else brewing here." "It is nothing Shan, we were just chatting about her classes,......and having a special mother daughter bonding time," Kaya tries to divert his attention. Shan laughs aloud and says, "You girls are trying to sideline me. I am taking you out for a movie tonight so be ready in time." "That is wonderful Dad, it is going to be a lot of fun," Nita gets excited about the movie as it has been a long time since the three of them went out to watch a movie together. Kaya smiles at them and gets up to leave for her office. Shan also leaves and Nita reaches out to her phone and dials Aman's number.

Chapter 17

Nita cannot wait to speak to Aman to let him know of her latest discovery and achievement which has left her dumbfounded, like a revelation of truth in a mystery, an enlightenment that has brightened her life after a long period of darkness. She calls him up and talks to him at an express speed with her words overlapping each other, "Aman, I need to tell you something, I have to meet you immediately, it is very important, I should have told you earlier but I have to......now....when can we meet.....and where?" "Calm down Nita, we can meet now at Maxing Garden. What is it that you want to tell me? Can we talk about it on phone now?" Aman asks her. "No, I want to tell you in person, it is very important," Nita tells Aman. Nita is extremely excited and cannot wait to be with Aman and let him know about Mini, her imaginary world, her mystic creations and the latest discovery of her life that has left her puzzled, amused and relieved at the same time. Aman is perplexed as he wonders what it is that Nita wants to talk about. They meet under the shade of the Magnolia trees at Maxing Garden after forty minutes. Aman sees Nita run towards him from the front gate of the garden and wonders what is it that she wants to tell him. "Mini is gone," Nita tells him in her incoherent voice as she is panting. "Mini?" Aman asks with various shades of confusion splashed on his face. Nita nods and smiles, "Yes, Mini is gone. She was me, I was her, we were us, you know like,......maybe twins,.........or an alter ego,........or just a reflection,........it is hard to explain but .....I,.......you,.....try to understand, Aman". Aman shakes his head and asks her to sit down and talk slowly and explain to him in detail so that he can understand her. "You know I talk to someone, I mean I used to talk to someone,....you may have noticed it too,.....I have been talking to myself all these years, it was not Mini, it was me, I was used to talking to

93

myself, my own hidden self that I found to be superior and more confident than me," Nita tries to explain to Aman with her expressive eyes talking in parallel with her. Aman is trying to comprehend her statements and nods his head as she talks. "Okay, so you have been talking to yourself. Yes, I have noticed you mumbling and winking in the air and I did hear the name Mini before. So you are trying to tell me that you had an imaginary person to talk to whom you had created yourself. Am I right?" Aman asks her. "Yes, you could say that and today I have realized that this person was none other than me. I and Mini are one and I do not need to speak to myself anymore as I have turned into a confident person, someone who can face the world alone. Is it not wonderful?" Nita looks at Aman with her dreamy eyes and a beaming smile of victory on her beautiful face.

Aman smiles and wonders how to react to Nita as it is a very unusual story that he has just heard which sounds absurd and a bit impossible, and rather preposterous. He finds it a little funny and is about to comment but his words get masked in the sound of the breeze blowing at high speed and he immediately realizes how important it was for Nita to overcome this problem of hers. Nita has renewed confidence with the understanding of herself that she has acquired today which has brought the glow of peace on her beautiful face. Aman understands how important it was for Nita to fight her drawbacks and today she is standing in front of him with the courage to acknowledge her shortfalls and talk about them with such confidence, he can see a different Nita standing there in front of him, a glowing soul very much at peace with her own existence. He does not want to undermine her sense of accomplishment but he wants to add to this confidence of hers and believes he needs to encourage her further so he appreciates her, "Nita, this is definitely wonderful news. I am so glad that you could fight yourself. I am glad that you have been able to find yourself, now I will not have to wait for you to finish your conversation with Mini before I can speak to you." Nita smiles and feels relieved as she had expected him to laugh at her and make fun of her stupidity. "I thought you would laugh at me and make fun of me," Nita tells Aman in a voice filled with respite and her eyes wide open with astonishment at his reaction. Nita is very much at ease seeing Aman's reaction and is thankful to God for giving her a friend who can understand her so well. "Oh, I could not have, I am able to understand your problem and why you felt the need to create a fence of Mini around you that could protect you, support you and make you feel at ease, I do understand you," Aman tells Nita in a comforting voice that puts Nita at greater ease. "Thanks Aman, you make me feel so much relieved. I am so blessed to have you as my best friend. You understand me so well, I was a little uncomfortable in telling you thinking that you may find my story stupid and consider me to be insane," Nita tells Aman with a smile which talks of the peace she has found both mentally and emotionally by disclosing her secret to Aman. "And so do you. You understand me the best Nita, you can hear me even when I am quiet," Aman replies.

It is a very happy moment for Nita as life has opened a new chapter in her life, a confident chapter which will help her move ahead in life towards her ambitions and designs of her life. Life has changed for the better for her and having a friend like Aman by her side is a benediction and the feeling that she loves the man who understands her is like the icing on the cake of her life. Nita has discarded the imaginary garb of Mini and she seems to have been reborn as Nita today, a rebirth, a reincarnation of her strength, her soul and her very individuality that has shaped up into a personality which is strong, attractive, bold and confident!!

Chapter 18

Mr. Sharma glides into the room with an air of excitement and announces the exhibition and sale event being organized by the Arts School to showcase the talent of its students from the painting, pottery and sculpture classes. The students are excited on hearing the news and get down to preparing their works for the exhibition, an opportunity to show their skills and talent to the world. The news about the exhibition sets the school in motion with each student putting in extra hours trying to perfect his or her exhibits with commotion in the corridors which are used as a much needed retreat by students after the day's hard work. Aman is ready after hours of slogging with his paints and brushes, ready and set for the exhibition with his works that are perfected to be put on display. He has his masterpiece and three more paintings on display at the exhibition for which the Arts School has invited top dignitaries from Art Galleries and Corporate Houses. Painting exhibits are in the central hall and pottery and sculpture exhibits are on display in the adjoining halls. Pam and other students have lined up their exhibits in the main hall of the Arts School where Aman's works are displayed in the centre. The students are busy rearranging their works to give them the best display at the exhibition, each one trying to find a better spot than the other, trying for a spot with higher visibility, deciding the angles of their displays to gain maximum attention from the audience, adjusting their works and readjusting to make them look best from all viewing angles. Some are reworking on their masterpieces to perfect them to win appreciation and admiration and also awards that would be announced at the end of the exhibition. Aman retouches his masterpiece with some brush strokes and plans to call Nita for her opinion on the painting before he strikes the imaginary bell to say, "I am ready". Nita is spellbound as she sees the painting of masks, a painting that contains the gist of all emotions within its colours and gives him her approval with a broad smile and a twinkle in her eyes. "This is surely going to win the award for the best painting made by any artist ever, and your other paintings are awesome too and will get you outstanding comments from the guests," Nita tells Aman in awe of the wonderful paintings she is beholding. Nita feels proud to be standing there, proud of his work, his achievements and his superior creative skills which translate with ease his innermost feelings into a painting, proud to be in love with him, a feeling that these are her attainments, her feats from being a part of his soul. Such is love, a feeling that nourishes you with the sensation that you can understand and feel one with your other half and become a part of another at the same time!!

Where there is love, there are negative energies too trying to counter love's goodness by the underhand scheming and plotting to destroy the good with evil intentions as life is never a bed of roses and where roses live thorns have to thrive in good abundance too. Pam is unable to see Nita admire Aman's work, each word of her admiration is a whiplash that leaves its mark on her soul. Her eyes run through all the exhibits and she is unable to control her envy when she sees Aman's paintings and her face fumes in anger and her heart burns with jealousy. "How can Aman be the best? He can never be as good as I am. My stain glass art is the best and should be at the centre stage. I will not let people look at Aman's work," Pam voices her jealousy and thinks of a plan to make people ridicule Aman's work, her mind's wickedness works all day long to scheme and plot against Aman. She meets Mr. Sharma and pleads for her work to be set in the centre of the room as her work is different and she feels glass will catch more attention from the guests. Mr. Sharma does not give in to her persuasion and reasons with her for keeping Aman's work in the centre, "Pam, you have to acknowledge that Aman's work is far superior to the stain glass art etchings made by you. We will have to let the display be as it is. Your work is visible and will be viewed before Aman's as it is on its left so you should actually not worry at all and, in fact, you should feel good about it." Pam is not convinced with Mr. Sharma's logic so she goes back to the class to execute her wicked plan while the students are waiting for Mr. Sharma in the main lobby. There is a rush of adrenalin through Mr. Sharma as he looks towards the main gate in anticipation of greeting the dignitaries as soon as they arrive at the school. The dignitaries arrive one after another and Mr. Sharma welcomes them and directs them to the auditorium where they assemble for a small presentation by the teachers before they are taken to the exhibition halls. The dignitaries are taken through half an hour presentation about the Arts School and the various art and other streams being taught at the school before they walk through the halls moving from one exhibit to the next with awe and adulation for the splendid works of art presented by the students. Rajat Gupta from the famous 'Pratyaksh' Art Gallery and Dewanji Junior from the reputed Dewanji Group of Companies are the most distinguished guests at the exhibition. Aman's eyes are searching for Nita as his soul feels incomplete without her presence and she is the only one who can provide him the much needed support that he requires today as it is a day of judgement, judgement of his work, his skills, his creativity and, above all, the judgement that will prove to him that he is no longer a failure in life. Aman is also waiting for his parents whom he has invited to see his exhibits and be with him on the day of judgement. It seems like a long wait before Nita appears with her tresses flowing and moving around in an attempt to cover her beautiful face. His parents reach in time for the exhibition and walk in with great pride as they are confident that they are going to witness a day filled with great comments about their son's paintings. Nita, Jagat and Sheela's presence gives Aman a sense of respite on knowing that he is not alone on this significant day of his life, he has them to support him if things do not turn out as expected and to cheer him if his work gets appreciated. He takes them inside the hall and introduces his parents to Mr. Sharma.

"Are you nervous Aman, I sure am, don't know what the experts will say," Nita asks Aman. "I am a little nervous today Nita, I am hoping that I should not get any negative comment, that would be hard to take," Aman tells Nita about his fears. Nita holds Aman's hand in her nervousness but smiles at Aman as a mark of reassurance. Simi and Ajay come in after some time and stand with Mr. Sharma and the other students. "Mom and Dad, this is Nita, my best friend and the most special one," Aman introduces Nita to Jagat and Sheela with a twinkle in his eyes which cannot escape their attention. His parents are happy to meet Nita and take an instant liking to her as she has the face of an angel that talks of her beautiful soul. Nita and Sheela start talking with each other and Aman is happy to see them bonding as Nita is soon going to be a part of his family.

Chapter 19

Dewanji Junior and Rajat Gupta are walking together admiring the awesome exhibits on display at the pottery section where the students have instilled life into clay to build incredible pieces of pottery, the traditional pots and vases are displayed in one section of the hall and the other section has modern art with abstract models of clay, a miniature of village life made with clay catches the maximum attention of the visitors as it has been painted with bright colours and looks like a real village. The next section is the hall with the painting art forms on display which excites Rajat Gupta's passion for art. The other guests are following Rajat Gupta and Dewanji Junior who are the guests of honour. Deep's work is being admired by the dignitaries and this invites anger and jealousy from Pam who cannot bear to see anyone else get appreciation from the guests. Rajat Gupta likes Deep's work and gives his views on his paintings to Deep and Mr. Sharma. Aman congratulates Deep on his success, "Great job Deep. Great going." Simi, Ajay, Nita and the other students also congratulate Deep who is feeling very excited on hearing Rajat Gupta's comments about his artwork. Dewanji Junior and Rajat Gupta walk together till they reach Pam's work. Pam runs up to stand behind them and waits for their comments with eagerness as her eyes are fixed on her painting and her ears wait for the comments from the guests. They spend the least time at Pam's exhibit which upsets Pam and she heaves a sigh in her frustration, her eyes are turning red and she clasps her hands together as she fidgets from one foot to the other. Next in line is Vijay's work which gets a good review from Dewanji Junior who admires his work and questions him about the theme of his sand art and the oil canvas paintings. Vijay explains his work to him and the other guests who have queued up in front of his exhibits. He is happy to hear good comments from the guests and the other students congratulate him. They walk towards Aman's work and that brings the smile back on Pam's face. Dewanji Junior's mobile phone rings and he moves out of the hall to take the call leaving Rajat Gupta alone to admire Aman's work.

Rajat Gupta runs through the canvas as he scans every dot in detail with his expert eyes, he is engrossed in exploring the painting with his eyes trying not to miss even the smallest dot on the canvas. There is a long silence followed by a deep breath and Rajat stands there for long inspecting the canvas from all angles, he reaches into his shirt pocket to pull out his spectacles and wears them to view a clearer image of the painting moving closer to the canvas and scanning it slowly from one end to the other, horizontally and vertically. He moves back a few steps to look at the canvas from a distance and then walks closer to it. Aman and Nita have been busy talking to Vijay, congratulating him, so they do not realize that the guests have moved to Aman's exhibits. "Aman, it is your turn now," Vijay tells Aman and gestures with his eyes in the direction of Aman's paintings. Aman quickly walks with Nita and his parents to his section of the exhibits and is shocked to see Rajat looking at his rough canvas. He quickly moves towards Rajat and tries to say something but Rajat moves his hand gesturing at him to remain silent as he does not want any distraction that would stop him from admiring the work in front of him. Mr. Sharma notices the canvas and turns to Aman in a state of shock, "What is this Aman? Where is your masterpiece? What is this canvas doing here?" he asks Aman. "I too am totally clueless Sir, I have no idea how this rough canvas got here, my mask painting was right here on display an hour ago and is nowhere to be seen now, I too am shocked to see this canvas here," Aman tells Mr. Sharma in his anguish with his mind in a total state of shock and angst at the turn of events. Nita is in a state of shock herself and she is unable to talk but her eyes are telling her pain as they have turned moist. She looks around and notices Pam smiling at them, a smile that speaks of her evil mission, her envy that has made her switch Aman's painting, a masterpiece with a rough sketch, downgrading her soul to the lowest possible level. Nita realizes that it is Pam's doing, her jealousy has overpowered her and led her to this level of degradation but she is more worried for Aman and what reaction would he get from the guests about his work. She looks at Aman and feels sorry for him as he is standing there distraught as a bird whose nest has been destroyed by the storm, a person whose very identity has been blown away by a catastrophic cyclone, his individuality has been blown to bits, torn away, just ruined, his eyes are filled with an emptiness that shocks Nita. Nita prays to God, "God, please don't let them ridicule Aman's work. Please let them overlook this canvas. I will not be able to see them mocking this canvas." Aman seems to be standing on the mouth of a volcano which is about to explode any minute to engulf him in the anger of its fuming lava and move him away, far far away, to a land where he will not have to see someone mocking his work, all his efforts have just been lapped up by a huge wave of misfortune and his hours and days of toiling on his masterpiece have been turned into dust within minutes, the world has taken a turn for the worst by masking his masterpiece with his rough canvas. Aman is unable to decipher how his masterpiece got switched with this one, his thoughts are clouded with extreme disappointment and his heart is filled with grief, tearing his heart and mind apart at this cruelty met out to him by the scheming minds of the world. Nita is looking at Aman with helplessness that speaks volumes of her love for him, the ability to feel the emotions of the other half of your soul, love that makes you feel the pain your other half is experiencing making your heart wrench and tear open and bleed. She shares his disappointment, grief and frustration as her heart tears apart at the grave situation faced by them. Nita holds Aman's hand to let him know he is not alone and the soft touch of Nita's hand is the much needed support that Aman wants at the moment. Aman tightens his grip on her hand in an effort to hold on to hope that things will just pass by and the clock will turn back to set things right but it does not, time has moved ahead and they have no other choice but to move forward with it. They are staring at Rajat who has frozen in the moment and his silence is killing them as he stands there screening the canvas, standing there in a trance, like a meditation in front of an idol, an immobile disposition that is making the onlookers impatient leaving them anxious about his declaration of his judgement. Jagat and Sheela are waiting patiently for Rajat to announce his results with hope in their hearts and prayers in their minds as their eyes are fixed on the canvas and on Rajat Gupta with a wish to hear great admiration for their son's work. Dewanji returns after taking his phone call and notices Rajat standing like a statue next to a canvas. He is curious to see what has got Rajat so engrossed and walks up close to the canvas.

"Whew, this is a beauty!! Phenomenal!! Amazing!! Awesome!! Brilliant!! I do not have words to describe this work, incredible!!" Dewanji exclaims as he looks at Aman's rough canvas and jumps up as he cannot contain himself. His expressions bring a confused look on Aman's face as there were no expectations of admiration in his mind which was prepared to hear snide remarks instead, a smile on Nita's lips to hear adulation for the love of her life, true happiness on Jagat's face to hear praise for his son, tears of joy in Sheela's eyes to know that his son's work has met with success, a relief on Mr. Sharma's forehead on knowing that the rough canvas has passed through and that too with flying colours and a shocking frustration on Pam's face leaving her totally defeated as her plans of defaming Aman have failed miserably.

Rajat breaks his long silence and responds to Dewanji as though he has been woken from a deep slumber. "It is indeed,……..a beauty! Indeed! This is what I call a masterpiece!! Look at the juxtaposition of the colours, the awesome shades used, the effect of shadows is brilliant and the theme and the thought surpasses art! I just love it! It has the definition of life and its various shades all packed on a single canvas. Brilliant!! Unbelievable!! Superlative!!" Rajat's remarks leave Aman, Sheela, Jagat, Nita and Mr. Sharma stunned as they look at each other and then at Rajat in their happiness which has poured in a deluge when it was least expected, a rainbow on a sunny afternoon with no clouds or rains. Aman tries to explain, "Sir, there must be some confusion, my mask painting has been…………,". Rajat cuts him short, "I know a masterpiece and I know art when I see it, who is the artist?" Rajat questions the students who have crowded around him to take a look at the piece of wonder that has left him fascinated beyond words. "I am,….. the artist," Aman says in his nervousness. Rajat looks at Aman in great admiration and wonder and shakes hands with him, looks at him again and hugs him, "You are the real artist man! You are amazing! I am buying this work and am buying all your works." Rajat's words leave Aman in a state of shock, a shock from happiness and Nita and Mr. Sharma shake hands with Aman as they congratulate him. Jagat and Sheela hug him and their happiness knows no bounds, a dream come true, their son has excelled in his art and has made them extremely proud. Dewanji Junior also shakes hands with Aman and pats his back, "Good work Aman! Excellent!" Mr. Sharma requests them to look at the painting of masks which he has noticed to be pushed behind the rough canvas and pulls it out from behind Rajat's masterpiece. Rajat and Dewanji look at the mask painting in awe and are speechless on seeing the ultimate work that is so superior that it leaves them spellbound. "I love this one too but the first one is still my favourite," Rajat remarks on seeing the mask painting. Rajat Gupta and Dewanji Junior look at his other works and find them to be unbelievable and there is a tussle between them as to who will buy which painting and there is an altercation between them. Mr. Sharma quickly offers to help them decide, "Why don't you bid for the works and the highest bidder can take the prize?"

Aman and Nita are amidst a cloud of emotional outburst as this is the happiest moment for them which has given life to their dreams, this is the ultimate appreciation that an artist can receive for his efforts, a moment that is taking them on cloud nine as they are totally dazed by the heavenly showers of happiness that are drenching them with extreme joy, a sense of total and final achievement that leaves them wondering if there is anything more to be wished for in life. Jagat and Sheela cannot hide their excitement and admiration for their son and they are clapping and cheering him like small children. Sheela holds Aman's hand in pride as Jagat looks at them with extreme adoration, the highest degree of happiness and pride has filled them with divine bliss. Mr. Sharma asks Rajat and Dewanji to bid for the paintings one by one as he calls the Principal Mrs. Choudhary to chair the auction. The hall is filled with guests who are cheering in excitement and students from all other streams of the school are gathering to witness the auction of Aman's paintings. The two bidders try to outbid each other and this leads to an exponential increase in the bid amount leaving Aman gaping at them in shocking disbelief. His parents cannot hide their emotions as the bids are moving from lacs of rupees to a crore for each painting with the students and guests cheering them and encouraging them to bid higher.

The bidding has turned into a battle of honour between Rajat and Dewanji as they try their best to keep bidding higher. The first painting goes for fifty lacs and the next two for one crore each leaving the crowd in a fit of ecstasy. The painting of masks, Aman's masterpiece fetches Aman one and a half crore but it is the rough canvas that gets the highest bid of three crores. The students and guests are cheering Aman loudly and the hall is echoing with the sound of their claps. Nita jumps up in her joy and hugs Aman, it is a long hug which speaks volumes of Aman and Nita's love for each other and defines the value they place on each other's success as they are bathing in their new found sunshine of glory. Sheela taps on Aman's shoulder and smiles as she says, "I need a hug too". Nita smiles and moves back as Sheela and Jagat hug Aman with their eyes shining with infinite pride and joy. It is a moment of truthful joy and happiness that has made so many people happy. Aman just cannot believe that this is happening for real, he thinks this is a dream and he will wake up soon to find that there is no one in the hall with him. He is surrounded by students who are cheering him as he is standing there in a trance and trying to acknowledge reality. Mr. Sharma walks up to Aman and hugs him and blesses him. "I am so proud of you Aman," Mr. Sharma smiles at Aman. Mrs. Choudhary, the Principal comes and shakes hands with Aman, "You have created history today Aman. The Arts School is so proud of you." Aman is delighted to hear her and cannot hide his excitement which is overflowing from his smile and eyes. "I will give credit to Mr. Sharma for helping me develop my techniques and giving me this opportunity to showcase my talent, he has been a great mentor, it would have been impossible to achieve this without his guidance," Aman tells Mrs. Choudhary as Mr. Sharma looks at them with tears in his eyes, tears of reaching the highest possible attainment with the unmatched success of his student. The world seems to be showering its blessings and admiration on Aman who has suddenly moved from being a 'nobody' to a 'name to be penned down in history'. Life has brought about a sudden change in Aman's life that has pulled him into the limelight within hours and of course with his undaunted and unrelenting efforts in perfecting his art. Dewanji Junior congratulates Aman and offers him a life time contract for advertisement and marketing features for his group and offers to fund his art gallery if he decides to set up one. Rajat Gupta tells Aman that he would like to buy his future works for his gallery and offers to sign a contract with him. Aman has bagged two prestigious contracts with Rajat Gupta and Dewanji Junior and that leaves him elated, shocked and confused. Life has brought too much for him in one go as heavens seem to be favouring him with their priciest gifts. Aman has suddenly moved into the spotlight within months of being mocked for his failures. Aman cannot wait to tell Ravi about this achievement. Jagat and Sheela are on cloud nine and Nita is standing mesmerized till she suddenly remembers Pam and tries to look for her.

Pam is standing in a corner burning in the fire of her anger and envy as she sees students congratulating Aman. "Pam, I hope you have realized by now that envy can get you nowhere. You had tried your best to ruin Aman's reputation but just look at what you have done, you have, in fact, helped him in the process. Your jealousy has proved to be self-destructive for you. Hope you have learnt your lesson for good and will not stoop so low ever again in your life," Nita hurls her spite at Pam. Pam is too angry and frustrated to speak as her forehead is filled with folds of her disgust and helplessness on her failed plan. Aman is looking for Nita and finds her with Pam. He hears a part of their conversation and understands that Pam is responsible for switching his paintings but he keeps his cool as it is a moment which needs to be celebrated and not wasted in these issues. He takes Nita's hand and tells her to forget what Pam has done. "Let us go and celebrate. Let her not spoil our day," Aman tells Nita. Nita is extremely angry with Pam and confused at Aman's forgiving nature and asks him, "How can you forgive her Aman? You cannot let her get away unscathed!" "She helped me make a lot of money today Nita, in fact, I should thank her for what she did," chuckles Aman and smiles at Nita. Aman winks at Nita and asks her to follow him.

"Aman, do you remember I had predicted that you will be famous soon and get billions for your art. I was right and things shaped up just the way they should have," Nita tells Aman. "Yes, you predicted it right. I did not think something as great as this could happen to me but it has. You had faith in me,……..thanks for having faith in my work and in me, Nita. It means a lot to me," Aman tells Nita as they walk towards the exhibits. They are soon with Jagat and Sheela who are happy to see them together. "I am going to build a studio for you Aman," Jagat tells Aman with pride. Aman cannot believe what he has just heard as Jagat had never favoured his taking up art as a profession but today he has offered to help build a studio for him which means a lot to him. Aman is elated at the thought of having his own studio where he can paint all through the day and live with his passion.

The school celebrates the great day with a party for the students. Aman has grown into the most sought after man within hours of the opening of the exhibition, life has pulled him out of a crowd to place him on a pedestal giving him a distinction which is for the favoured ones, ones who are life's own favourite. Life has reached the peak of its design for Aman today as he has finally stepped out of the shadows of failed attempts and moved into the light of his own success which is shining brightly on him.

Sheela invites Nita and her parents to Jagat Mansion for a party to celebrate Aman's success which leaves Nita delighted. Nita and her parents enter Aman's home and Nita's future home for the first time and are greeted by Aman and his parents with great warmth and acceptance of Nita in their family. It is a celebration to remember with esteemed guests from the reputed business houses of Saloni, the faculty and students of the Arts School, Rajat Gupta and Dewanji Junior and relatives and friends of the Dutt Family. Aman introduces Nita and her parents to all his friends and relatives and of course to his best friend Ravi who is elated to meet her. "Aman is always lost in your thoughts and cannot stop talking about you," Ravi tells a beaming Nita who is extremely happy to know what Aman thinks about her. "You two make a great couple,….I would say an extraordinary couple,…..just made for each other,…you know how they say marriages are made in heaven,….I think yours has been made by God Himself!" Ravi tells them bringing an extreme sense of joy to them making their evening extra special. Kaya and Shan seem to like Aman a lot and speak to him at length which makes Nita very happy as her parents' approval of her love means a lot to her. Aman's success marks a new beginning in his life which has a promising future that is designed to bless him with extraordinary attainments.

Chapter 20

---✦✦✦---

Six months fly away in no time and it is the month of October and Nita has to keep the promise made to her parents and it is not difficult for her to take over the business now as she is a very different person from the timid little girl that she was six months ago with her confident look that says she is ready to face the world and her new assignment in life. Aman has been busy at his studio making great masterpieces for 'Pratyaksh' Art Gallery. He has also been getting orders from other Art Galleries of repute keeping him totally engaged at his studio. The world has been kind to both of them making them flow with its design to the 'finish line' of their achievements which they had set out for about six months ago. They have been fortunate to taste success soon in their lives as many spend years searching for success and are still unable to find it. God and life have been kind to them as they seem to be the chosen ones who have been made to emerge out of their shadows in a short period of time. Their bond of friendship and love has grown stronger with the passage of time as they have shared their success and pains and walked together through time with faith in each other.

It is October and time for Nita to take over the travel agency business her parents have named 'Navigatory' and it is a day of pride and happiness for her parents as they accompany her to her office where they perform a 'puja' before Nita settles in her cabin. The huge corridors, glass cabins, the clicking of heels and the noise from the keyboards do not haunt her anymore, in fact, she does not even notice these trivial things as she enters her cabin. Life takes a new turn with Nita wearing an independent glow on her face to understand the business world with the help of a dedicated and hardworking team of enthusiastic employees. She calls Aman to give him the news of her taking over her business and Aman's voice is filled with joy as he congratulates her. "I have a staff of six to help me at my office, you must come over and see my office," Nita tells Aman in a cheerful voice. "Of course I will be there soon Nita, I have to see your office. And how about your visit to my studio? It has been a long time since you came here and admired my paintings. I hope it is not 'out of sight out of mind'. Hope your feelings for me have not changed with your new business. I will not let you switch me with your new business," Aman says in a teasing tone to Nita. "Aman, how can you be so mean? I will be there soon, have to see all your paintings. My feelings can never change, bye for now, need to get back to work, I will meet you tomorrow evening at your studio, okay," Nita replies to Aman. "Okay, I will be waiting for you, bye," Aman tells Nita and looks at his mobile phone with love and admiration as though he is looking at Nita and his mind flies to the days at the Arts School to reminiscence the days spent with Nita and her constant admiration for his work, the look on her face when she liked his painting, her excitement on seeing every new work of his, the sadness on her face when she had to leave from his class, her beautiful eyes that always told him to keep moving ahead, the sparkle in her eyes that said she loves him to the extent of madness and her flying hair that her fingers kept playing with and hid her beautiful face whenever she got annoyed with him. Nita is settling down in her office with her thoughts racing to Aman and making her restless as she misses him and wants to be with him as soon as she possibly can. She knows she cannot see him till the next evening and that makes her miserable and she tries hard to get back to her work and focus on her first meeting which is difficult but she forces herself to work on the presentation for her first meeting for the day and for her new career. "Oh, Aman, please let me work, I need to complete this presentation, just try to stop entering my thoughts for a little while," Nita tells herself trying to make her mind focus on her work.

Nita has to meet her first client, Sagar Rai from the Sagar Group of Hotels, a man with multiple hotels across the country, implying the golden opportunity for exploring travel requirements for him, his staff and his guests and Nita gets busy preparing for a grand presentation, her first one, to grab this deal and start her business account rolling for Navigatory. She rehearses her presentation several times, perfecting it to make a mark at her first meeting with her new found confidence and a hope that things will materialize to her advantage. Sagar Rai is a young man, contrary to Nita's expectations of meeting an old man, a man of class, polished, with mannerisms exuding his richness and a polite disposition with a soft voice that has the hint of maturity in it as he speaks to Nita and his eyes stare out of the window with little interest in Nita's presentation. Nita continues, in spite of seeing his disinterest, with the sole aim to convince him to give her the contract for his hotels, some of the hotels, if not all. "You are new to this business, Ma'am, and we have a huge clientele that we have built with our goodwill over the last decade and we cannot risk handing our customers to a newcomer, I have a reputation at stake, I don't think I would like to take any risks," Sagar Rai tells her gently with a fake smile on his face, a smile that says, "You may leave now as I have work to attend to and you are wasting my precious time", as he looks at her for the first time and nods his head as a reconfirmation of his statement. Nita smiles and her gaze moves to her laptop and back to Sagar, gaining her calm and retaining her poise in spite of the difficult situation at hand, "I am sure you would have had a first time at least once in your career,......we all do, there must have been a first deal which you managed with a flair of expertise,...I too will,.....only if I get a chance. I was hoping to start my business career with you and make it a lifetime contract with the excellent services of my company. I hope you could reconsider your decision and give me a chance to work with your company. You could give me a one-time contract and decide if my firm is able to live up to your expectations or not." Sagar listens to her patiently while his eyes are focussed on his watch as time is precious for successful people and he wants Nita to realize it. He nods his head again and says, "I have thought about it and my decisions are always final. I hope you will understand me and excuse me as I need to leave for a meeting now." Sagar gets up and calls his secretary to summon his chauffeur as Nita packs her laptop and collects her failed attempt gently, smiles at Sagar elegantly and walks out gracefully thanking him for his time. She is a little disappointed as this was her first presentation but she remembers her father's advice, "Nita, you may not find immediate success in your business but things will fall in line as long as you do not quit trying." Nita smiles as she hears her father's words echo in her mind and she walks out of Sagar Rai's office with her hair flying carelessly and hiding her pretty face. She suddenly stops with a spark in her thoughts that seem to have generated a brilliant idea, turns around with sheer determination and goes back to Sagar Rai's office with a hope that he would not have left for the meeting, jumping into the lift to come face to face with Sagar Rai who is stepping out of the lift,...whew,.... almost a collision that got averted!

Sagar is surprised to see her again and gives her a quizzical glance and looks at her unkempt hair that is flying in all possible directions to cover her face which is red from running, a sight that could be most displeasing for someone who is trying to bag her first contract. "I will just take a minute and no more. You could take our services for a month for free and if you are satisfied with the quality you can give us the contract else I quit bothering you," Nita says in one breath with her fingers adjusting her hair moving them behind her ears while Sagar is caught unawares and forced to give a thought to her proposal as his own travel bills run into millions for a month and then there are additional bills for his staff, the customers pay from their own pockets so that is not concerning for Sagar at this point of time when he has been offered such a lucrative deal. The two are standing in the hotel lobby in silence for a few minutes, total silence that is killing. Silence has a peculiarity to scream when there is a need for words to be heard and spoken, a sharp sense of piercing the air in its wake. Silence screams as Nita waits for an answer from Sagar who is lost in deep thought, feeling he is giving away to her persuasion though he does not like changing his decisions as they are always final. Sagar finally breaks the silence, "I hope you know there are millions at stake here, you could face bankruptcy." Nita knows what she is getting into and she replies with confidence that makes a mark on Sagar for the first time, "I am aware of the consequences, I have nothing to lose as you will be giving me the contract after a month." Sagar nods in agreement for the first time and smiles, a genuine one this time and Nita knows she has bagged the deal!

She finds it difficult to hide her excitement and keeps a straight face while moving out of Sagar's office like a thorough professional not being affected by any situation that she has been faced with but jumps up in joy as she reaches her car. She immediately calls her father, "Dad, I got the deal for Sagar Group of Hotels, I am very excited." Shan is elated to hear her. "Congratulations! Excellent! Great to hear this news, God bless you daughter, hope you keep getting more such contracts and Navigatory makes a fortune, I am really impressed. Did you tell your mother about it?" Shan asks her as his pride is making his face glow and his happiness at his daughter's success is filling his face with smiles. "I have to call her Dad, I thought of calling you first," Nita tells him and dials her mother's number immediately. "Mom, I got the deal, I did it," Nita tells her mother who gets up from her seat and almost shouts in her excited voice, "Lovely news Nita! Congratulations! I am so proud of you. So happy for you, this calls for a celebration. Did you tell your Dad about it? What was his reaction? I am sure he must be feeling really very proud. I don't think I will be able to work today in this state of extreme frenzy." "Thanks Mom, I did call him, he was very happy, and so am I, it feels great," Nita tells Kaya and calls Aman with a blissful smile appearing on her lips as she sees his name and number on her mobile screen.

Love makes you find happiness in every little thing connected with the one you love and everything related to Aman makes Nita flow into his dreamy thoughts making her walk into a beautiful world overflowing with celestial happiness. "Hi, Aman, I got my first deal, …my first contract, …the guy was apprehensive first but I managed to convince him," Nita tells Aman excitedly. "Wow, that is great, congratulations dear, this is a moment of great pride, I feel so happy for you, …we should celebrate this with a nice dinner,…love you,….feel so great talking to you and hear excitement and happiness in your sweet voice, it makes my day special," Aman tells Nita with joy, pride and love in his voice. "Thanks Aman, I will be meeting you soon. I feel very relieved after getting this deal. It sets the clock in motion for Navigatory and I will be able to manage more contracts based on the success of this contract. It is great to hear your voice,….love you,…I will be able to manage the rest of my day after hearing your voice,….will call you later,…take care,….love you," Nita tells Aman with her heart yearning to meet him. Aman gets back to his painting but his brush strokes move in a confused state as his heart misses Nita and wants to meet her soon, a feeling that makes love grow stronger with every passing moment.

Chapter 21

Nita keeps her promise and is at Aman's studio the next evening. She cannot stop admiring his works and Aman cannot stop admiring her. "Wow, each painting is a masterpiece in itself. Aman, your works have so much life in them, they speak to me. You leave me amazed with every painting that you create. You are an amazing artist and know how to sweep me off my feet with your incredible paintings which have highly commendable themes. I wonder what inspires you to create such magnificent and extraordinary works. I am blessed to have you by my side. The artist in you will always bring beauty in our lives. These paintings are to be treasured and cherished, don't know how you can part with them when you sell them to the Art Galleries, I would not be able to part with them if I were you," Nita is awestruck as her eyes light up on seeing Aman's works. "I have to make a living, Nita. I have to earn to make a home for you soon. I have you to treasure and cherish forever so I do not mind parting from them. I will not be able to part from you, ...ever, ..., and you are my inspiration for my work,....each time I am lost and unable to think of a theme, I just close my eyes and think about you and the themes just come to me with your thoughts in the backdrop,....I miss you with every brush stroke and that brings the love and life and a soul, as you have named it, in my paintings, you make my work extraordinary, it is your love that reflects in my works and gives them the majestic charm which flows into its theme,.....I do not think I will be able to paint if I did not have you in my thoughts," Aman gets emotional as he speaks to Nita. Nita has tears in her eyes as she hears Aman speak with so much love for her, she is touched and feels contented to hear him talk about her with such possessiveness. "Will you make a painting of me?" Nita asks Aman who shakes his head in refusal. "No, I do not want anyone to see your painting. I have painted you on my heart and my soul and that is where you will stay. If I ever make a painting of you it will stay in my room where no one can see it. You know I am too possessive about you," Aman's response delights Nita who feels fortunate to have him in his life.

It is a beautiful moment with Nita and Aman lost in each other's eyes when Ravi walks into the studio. "Now I know why you had asked me not to come over today," Ravi accuses Aman teasingly. Aman looks at him sheepishly and Nita giggles on hearing him tease Aman. Aman attempts to introduce Nita to Ravi who immediately remarks, "I know she is Nita, your lady love, I recognized her instantly, we met at your house, I can see a smile on Aman's face and tell that he is either thinking of you or is with you." Nita smiles at Aman and feels on top of the world to know that she and her thoughts can make Aman smile, it means a lot to her.

Ravi asks them to join him for dinner and the three of them dine at a Chinese restaurant close by. Ravi manages to bring them closer by asking Nita if Aman has proposed to her or not. "I know he must have forgotten to even ask you, the mind of an artist is crazy, he must have proposed to you in his thoughts and just forgotten about it,…did'nt you do that Aman,……. proposed to Nita in your dreams and forgot to actually propose to her," Ravi teases Aman again. Nita looks questioningly at Aman and Aman proposes to her instantly, "Nita, will you marry me?" Nita feels uneasy with the sudden question and does not know how to respond to him and looks at him in her surprise. Ravi is looking at both of them, shaking his head in disappointment on not getting any response from either of them. Nita's eyes sparkle in a few moments as she realizes that Aman has actually proposed to her, a question that she has been waiting for all these months bringing a sudden outburst of happiness in a large overdose that she is unable to contain and starts crying.

Ravi has been a great friend to Aman and helped him at the most important junctures of his life by making him join the Arts School where he met both Nita and immense success and now helping him propose to Nita. "The two of you need to get married soon," Ravi declares as Nita and Aman look at each other with an ocean of love overflowing from their eyes, hearts and souls. Aman nods and Nita asks Aman to wait for her to settle in her business before they go ahead and tie the knot as she needs to fulfill her promise to her parents who have great expectations from her. Aman is a very understanding person and knows Nita needs time to prove her worth to her parents by making her business prosper, he remembers the day she spoke of her drawbacks and knows how important it is for her to grow her business and make her parents proud and he too is waiting for her to make him proud by emerging a winner in this fight of hers. He agrees to wait for her but Ravi gives them a maximum time of one year. "Nita just take only an year and no more, Aman and you need to get married soon, I need to arrange for your wedding, I cannot wait to open the champagne at your wedding reception," Ravi gives them the ultimate deadline and Nita and Aman agree. It is a beautiful, joyful and wonderful night that has brought meaning to their relationship and Nita and Aman are thankful to Ravi for helping them take the decision to get married and have a life with happiness ever after. They feel fortunate to have a good friend like Ravi in their life who can help them when they need it the most.

Nita tells Aman about Sagar and the deal that she has offered him making Aman a little worried for her. "Are you sure about it? How will you manage the funds? Anyways I am there to support you with finances whenever you need them but this guy may not be taking you for a ride,......a month of free service and no contract at the end, ...you know what I mean," Aman says to her with concern in his voice. Nita is happy to know Aman is there to support her but she has reserve funds that her parents have given her and she knows she will be able to manage the deal and convince Sagar for the contract.

Nita and her staff set out with the sole aim to impress Sagar Rai and his staff with world class services, scoring high with their promptness, managing bookings on good flights for them and offering best vehicles for local travel with top class chauffeurs. Sagar knows Nita is creating a great impression with all efforts to overawe him and he is moving with the flow of life which is dominated by his doting grandmother Karuna Rai, a lady of absolute royalty, small and frail with fine wrinkles across her beautiful face that has aged gracefully with her. Sagar knows he is getting floored by the efforts made by Navigatory and he does not openly admit to the fact that his decision to refuse Nita the contract the first time was not right but he does plan to give her the contract for Sagar Group of Hotels soon.

Chapter 22

Sagar and Karuna are having their dinner at their palatial bungalow in Saloni Hills in a luxurious neighbourhood on the Saloni Hills running parallel to Aseem Mountains. "How is your new hotel coming along Sagar?" asks Karuna. "It is almost ready," replies Sagar as he drifts to the thoughts of his upcoming hotel. "Good, and what about your plans for marriage, I think Mr. Shah's daughter is the most suitable girl for you," Karuna catches Sagar unawares as this is one question that he likes to avoid at all times. Sagar coughs a little to divert his grandmother's attention from the topic of his marriage but Karuna does not give in so easily. "Or do you have someone else in mind?" she asks him in an indifferent but assertive tone. Sagar looks at her grandmother and shakes his head and looks at his bowl of rice, there is a blast of fresh air that blows in from the window, the white grains of rice suddenly turn into two dark brown eyes peeping at him leaving him spellbound, he sees a face covered with hair and a hand trying to move the hair away. "Why am I thinking about Nita?" Sagar questions himself with a puzzled look covering his handsome face that is lost in her thoughts and his mind is confused, unable to understand what is happening to him, a sudden turn of events that sees him confronting his innermost feelings that are causing him severe heartache. "Why? Why is she clouding my mind? What is wrong with me?" Sagar struggles with his mind to find an answer to his distressing questions that are baffling him. Karuna is staring at her grandson gauging his thoughts as she takes the last bite from her plate. "Well, I need an answer soon and I can see you are ready with the answer. Let me know soon as I want to see your wedding before God calls me back home," Karuna orders Sagar and leaves for her room while Sagar is still at the table, in the middle of his dinner, petrified and dazed, the feeling growing on him is new which is splashing itself across the room, the rays from the moon are caressing his face with love which is slowly lighting up with an extreme sense of joy creating ripples of smiles in his life. "I need to meet her soon and let her know, this is making me crazy,....I am going crazy,.....I am,......I really am,....I am in love with Nita," Sagar confesses his love to himself and runs to the terrace to behold the beautiful night, the skies are overflowing with the love emanating from his soul which is wrapped in joy and the brightness of the moon is special, a brightness he has never seen before, the moon is sharing the joy of his love and congratulating him for finding the most beautiful feeling of the world by walking out from behind the clouds that are lining the skies since the evening! Sagar thanks the skies and the moon for standing beside him in his moment of celestial happiness as his heart yearns to meet Nita and confess his love to her, behold the expression on her beautiful face and hear her say, "I love you too". Sagar is awake all night giving company to the bright moon and admiring the twinkling stars that have made a graceful appearance in the sky with the clouds moving away to another land. It is a memorable night for Sagar, the night that has changed his life swaying him into a world of joy, the supreme feeling of love pouring from the heavens in an overflow of exuberance in this night of heavenly bliss!

Sagar reaches Navigatory early next morning and waits in the parking lot for Nita to arrive with his heart lost in her thoughts and his mind rehearsing the lines he has to say to her to confess his love to her. It is an endless wait as the sun takes extra hours to appear on the horizon as it is the guest of honour today bringing the most important day for Sagar in its wake. Nita arrives after a wait of hours, her black tresses flowing behind her, her pretty dark brown eyes gazing at the signboard that says 'Navigatory' in dark blue font on white background, her feet moving gracefully on the pavement of Sagar's heart as she enters her office. Sagar is relieved to see her, relieved to be able to open his heart to her and admire her beautiful eyes and tresses as she looks at him in surprise and behold her beautiful smile as she accepts her love for him. Sagar follows Nita into her office and surprises her, making her jump literally from shock to see him in her office unannounced at nine thirty in the morning. "Hi, how are you?

Hope everything is okay. I mean,...I did not know you were coming to meet me today," Nita says in her surprise. "I too was not aware I was coming here,....I just thought of meeting you,......to let you know,......to,......to give you feedback about the experience of hiring your firm," Sagar makes an excuse for coming over, unable to tell her the real purpose of his visit, his heart is in his mouth as he suddenly feels too nervous and words refuse to help him let her know his love for her. Nita is still surprised and unsettled at seeing him there, trying to make him feel at ease, "That is great. Please take a seat. I am eager to know how you feel about our firm." Sagar is annoyed with himself for keeping his feelings hidden within his heart, his eyes try to catch hers but in vain, his hands fidget and play with the paper weight on the table in front and his voice is strange even for his ears that are hearing words that do not speak out the present thoughts of his heart. "I am very impressed, really very impressed with your staff and services, they are absolutely excellent, great, I was,.....I was wrong in passing a judgement about you as a beginner when we first met. I want to enter into a contract with Navigatory for all travel requirements for all my hotels, all hotels across the country and for the hotels that would come up in future too. I will be paying you for all the services taken by my company in the last two weeks, I cannot........take anything for free, I never do, please send me all the bills and we will settle them immediately," Sagar tells Nita as she looks at him dumbstruck. "Thanks, thanks so much for your feedback and I am really very happy that you liked the services. It means a lot for my staff, they have put in a lot of hard work in making things work. I also appreciate your clearing the bills, I will have them mailed to you today itself, thanks for everything," Nita says as she is very much relieved on hearing Sagar talk about clearing the bills and delighted to get the contract for his company which will help her get further contracts from other clients based on the credibility of this contract. It is a day of excitement for Nita and she cannot wait to call up her parents and Aman and let them know of her first real success at her business.

Sagar is anxious and disappointed for not being able to talk to Nita, his wait for hours for her in the morning has been in vain, a feeling of frustration with himself for falling prey to fears of rejection that stopped him from baring his heart open to her to read his love for her, he is dismayed and returns disheartened.

Nita is joyous but her happiness is masked with a strange feeling of confusion on Sagar's changed behaviour and attitude, witnessing a very different person who does not cease to amaze her with his curious antics and ambiguous disposition. Shan and Kaya and Aman are delighted to know about Nita's accomplishment and their voice on the phone has a tone of pride with the extreme elation from her achievement that is definitely an arduous task for a beginner, a contentment that things are falling in place and the road to success is not too far, great exhilaration on the triumphant victory that is a mark of an award for hard work and pure dedication and sincerity. Nita calls for a meeting with her staff to congratulate them and celebrate their first contract that has created history in the books of Navigatory.

Sagar returns in his misery and plans to return to Nita and speak his heart out, let her know what she means to him, make her feel special, let her know the place she holds in his life, sweep her off her feet with his confession and bring a smile on her pretty face and propose marriage to her, yes marriage, he is thinking marriage with her, love has turned him into a new person, a person who cannot hold his feelings, a person who is restless and miserable being away from her, the love of his life who means the world to him.

Chapter 23

Nita and Aman are working really hard to find success in their lives to make them worthy of what they had desired from life. They toil for long hours at work and share their escapades with each other at the end of each day to ensure that none of them is left out from the happenings in the other's life. They see a mentor in each other and try their best to give each other good advice to help tide over every obstacle that appears in the path of their life. Ravi is their support in all times whether good or bad and this adds to their confidence and motivation to know that they have someone to look up to when in need. Life is moving ahead as per its design for them and things start falling in place gradually to lead them to their destinations.

"Aman, Simi and Ajay are going to get married next week, is it not wonderful?" Nita tells Aman excitedly. "Wow, two weddings next week," Aman replies. "Two weddings? Who else is getting married?" Nita asks Aman. "You just mentioned Simi and Ajay are getting married so we have to attend both their weddings, don't we?" Aman asks Nita who is both shocked and amused at his comment and bursts into peals of laughter. "Aman, you must be joking. Simi and Ajay are marrying each other so there is only one wedding next week," Nita giggles as she speaks to Aman. "Oh, I get it now. Hey, I did not know that they were seeing each other. When did this happen?" Aman asks Nita. "I think it was in the Arts School almost towards the time when our course was getting over. They were spending a lot of time together and helping each other with the course, I guess they must have fallen in love then. I know they have been together since they passed out from the Arts School. I have always seen them together and believed they were made for each other," Nita tells Aman who is busy mixing some colours on his palette. "Ah ha, so that is their story. Good that they will soon be married. Then they can come as a couple to our wedding," Aman says in a loving tone to Nita who smiles and Aman can feel her smile through his phone, a smile that can make his day. "My soul feels at so much peace when it senses your happiness Nita," Aman tells Nita making her feel delighted to hear his feelings for her. "Yes, I too feel so calm and contended when I sense you are happy," Nita tells him in her dreamy voice. "And I can hear you even when you are quiet," Aman tells her as she smiles again on hearing his voice and feels blessed to have him in her life.

Love has filled their lives with a divine sense of achievement that tells them that there is nothing more left to be achieved in life. Love has the quality of bringing a sense of accomplishment that creates a dreamy aura around the people in love leaving them rejoicing in the heavenly bliss of the glory of immense happiness. Nita and Aman are also rejoicing in this divine glory that comes from their love for each other that binds their souls into one. Simi and Ajay's wedding is another story of love that Nita and Aman witness, a grand celebration that makes them want to get married soon. Simi and Ajay are dressed like a prince and princess and Nita finds the celebration to be out of a fairy tale. "Aman, I want us to get married with a fairy tale theme," Nita tells Aman as she dreams of herself dressed as a bride and Aman dressed as the groom walking on a cloud with angels surrounding them. "Anything you want, anything," Aman assures Nita with a smile that talks of his commitment to do anything that would make Nita happy and bring a smile on her pretty face. Their eyes are narrating their love for each other which is spreading its wings to bring happiness all around and bringing with it a realization for them that they should not wait any more to get married. "Look at them Aman. I have never seen them so happy before. Ravi was right, we should not take long to decide our wedding date," Nita tells Aman and Aman looks at Nita with his dreamy eyes that agree with her without the need for words. Aman nods and decides to meet her parents soon.

Life generally does not move the way we would want it to, it has its own twists and turns and its path can take any deviations or lead uphill or downhill as per its design which is always complicated in its simplicity. Aman and Nita soon get busy with their work and the decision to tie the knot takes a back seat as they think about it often but do not get to talk about it. Their work is too hectic to let them think about anything else as marriage of successful souls in love is definitely better than marriage of souls in love searching for success as the scope for arguments from shortfalls is greater in the second case. Life has probably designed their path to be of two successful souls who will get married later in life. Success, however, does not always get defined by the fat bank balances a person has or the plush mansions a man lives in or the luxurious cars a lady drives or the designer brands one wears. Success has another meaning too, a meaning of the sense of highest contentment from walking with someone else, holding their hands to the podium of their success. It is easy to succeed with hard work but helping someone achieve success is another feat which is not common. This is the highest degree of success when you can hold someone's finger and help the person cross the bridge from failure to success and clap for another person's achievement with tears of happiness flowing down from your cheeks that are lit up and swollen with immense joy. This must be the joy that God feels when His beings walk through the life designed by Him for them and find success!!

Chapter 24

Sagar has been unsuccessful in his attempts of declaring his love to Nita in the several meetings he has had with her, his words seem to find refuge in his heart and refuse to divulge to Nita who is running the travel agency business successfully with reputed clients from Saloni and nearby locations. She has been able to establish the business well in a short period of time with her sheer hard work and determination which comes from her confidence that empowers her with extreme faith in herself to make things happen and show great results. Aman is a man of high reputation whose work is much in demand from Art Galleries across the country as his unique art of blending shades has become very popular and sought after by connoisseurs of art who flock him with big orders for his priceless creations. His work and reputation have formed a great goodwill with his clients that fetches him exorbitant sums for his works leaving no room for wants or needs. Nita and Aman are tasting success with the passage of time as their hard work is getting translated into multiple achievements for them and life seems to have a calm sense of contentment but not complacence as their hearts' desire to better themselves with every feather in their caps is growing like a constant flame which makes them push themselves to reach out beyond their own limitations to touch the skies of new attainments.

Nita's business is growing gradually and with growth comes extra workload creating the need for more people making Navigatory advertise for new staff. Numerous applications start flowing in daily and Nita's manager Jugnu is busy interviewing candidates to shortlist them. There seems to be a dearth of jobs in Saloni as Navigatory sees numerous candidates walking in for the interview daily. Her manager Jugnu manages to shortlist some candidates after three days whom Nita has to meet to finalize the most appropriate ones for the job. Nita feels proud to get this opportunity to interview people for her office as this is something new that she has not done before. She has to meet five candidates today whom Jugnu has shortlisted and she has a strange feeling remembering how she had failed miserably at several job interviews and run away from the last one which reminds her of Mini and brings a smile on her face. She starts talking to the candidates and is impressed by Jugnu's selection which is good making it difficult to take a decision on the most suitable candidate for the job.

The fourth candidate walks in nervously and stammers as she answers Nita's questions. Mona, the short little fat girl who looks at the world through the glass of her spectacles stammers again as Nita tries to comfort her. "Mona, it is okay, take your time, you can have some water and answer my questions, feel at ease," Nita tries to make Mona comfortable as she sees her past through Mona. Mona has become a crystal ball that shows Nita her past, present and future; the trembling past that left Nita nervous, a confident present that gives Nita the bold disposition to handle any situation with ease and a bright future with Aman that brings a smile on her face as she drifts into his thoughts only to be brought back to the present by her mobile phone that rings sharply to distract her focus from the love of her life. Nita catches Jugnu smirking as Mona tries to speak and she looks at him angrily and gestures at him. Jugnu's smirk vanishes immediately on reading Nita's facial gesture. Mona leaves and they meet the last candidate. Jugnu has liked the last candidate and asks Nita if he can send her the offer letter. "No, I want Mona for this job," Nita tells Jugnu who is totally baffled by her statement. "Mona,.......Ma'am,.....are you sure?" Jugnu attempts to reconfirm Nita's decision. "Yes, I want Mona to work for us, she will be an asset to our agency," Nita replies to Jugnu who gapes at Nita in utter shock. Nita nods her head again and Jugnu complies with her orders though he thinks that she is acting irrationally. "What has got into her mind? Why does she want to keep the least capable of the lot?" Jugnu grumbles as he calls Mona to let her know that she has been selected for the job. Mona cannot believe her ears as she did not expect to be selected after having fumbled through the interview. It is a dream come true for her and she joins Navigatory the very next morning. She tip toes to Nita's cabin in a state of fright to express her gratitude to her for giving her this job with her heart thumping and her feet trembling. Nita looks up from her laptop and notices a nervous Mona trying to balance herself as she fidgets from one foot to the other. "I,......I,........wanted to thank you for giving me this job, Ma'am," Mona speaks in a feeble voice as her heartbeat increases with her nervousness. "You don't have to thank me but you will need to do as I tell you to," Nita remarks as she tries to calm her down. "Do not be afraid of anything, I know things do not seem very normal and the walls might be closing in on you and the world must be scheming to grab you but there is no need to worry at all as nothing that you fear will happen. You just have to take your seat and start working with total concentration on your work. Just think that no one exists in the office and you will find it easy to work," Nita talks to Mona from her experience as Mona looks at her in total shock to hear her talk of her fears. "How does she know how I feel? Is she a sorceress? Or can she read my mind? How does she exactly know what I am going through?" Mona wonders as she nods and replies to Nita with her heartbeat increasing at a breakneck speed. "Sure Ma'am, I will, ..., thanks," Mona comes out of Nita's cabin and takes her seat to comply with Nita's directions while her mind is still confused with Nita's remarks. She is terrified to be surrounded by people in the office but keeps working as a sign of gratitude to Nita who has shown confidence in her and probably in her abilities too.

Chapter 25

Sagar is taking a stroll in his garden taking a decision to disclose his feelings to Nita and not give in to his fears of rejection or hesitation to know her reaction which he would not bear to hear to be negative and decides to meet her and let her know! An hour later Sagar walks into Navigatory surprising the staff and Nita alike with his unanticipated visit and an exceptionally anxious stance. "Nita, I need to speak to you," Sagar tells Nita with great confidence and determination as his feelings are about to pour out in a stream of words which he is holding on to with great difficulty. Nita is looking at him waiting to hear him out as she senses something unusual about his stance that is unlike his usual self. "Yes, please take a seat and let me know," Nita says to him. Sagar is looking at her with love in his eyes and high hopes in his heart, a strange feeling engulfs him as he tries to speak to her.

There is a click of the doorknob and Nita smiles as she sees Aman walk into her cabin bringing an instant outburst of happiness and cheer on her face as she gets up to greet him. "Hi, Aman, this is Sagar Rai from the Sagar Group of Hotels, and Sagar this is Aman Dutt, the famous celebrity artist and my best friend," Nita introduces them. Aman and Sagar shake hands and gauge each other and a silence follows as Aman and Nita exchange glances that speak of their immense love for each other and Sagar sits there with his eyes glued on Nita. "Sorry, Sagar, you were saying something before Aman came in, sorry for the interruption, please continue," Nita asks Sagar who is at a loss of words as his love is to be shared only with the one he loves and Aman is another occupant in the room who makes his disclosure to Nita impossible. Sagar decides to make some excuse for his visit and notices Aman whose eyes are twinkling as he looks at Nita with a gaze that says that she means the world to him, making Sagar uncomfortable as he cannot bear to see someone look at Nita with an admiration that is beyond the limits of pure friendship. "I can come later if you are busy Nita," Aman asks Nita. "Yes, you must leave us alone and let me speak to her," thinks Sagar who wishes and prays for Aman to leave him alone with Nita but his wish remains unfulfilled and prayers unanswered as Nita tells him to stay back. "It is okay Aman. Sagar, I hope we can discuss now, I am sure we will not take long, Aman is actually worried that we may be late for the opening of his new studio," Nita tells Sagar. "I am okay, we can meet again if you are getting late," Sagar tells Nita. "No, it is okay, you two can finish your meeting while I wait outside for Nita," Aman tells them and walks out of Nita's cabin giving some respite to Sagar who is desperately trying to get some time alone with Nita to speak to her. "Sagar, Aman is a very nice person and a great artist," Nita has a starry eyed gaze as she continues talking about Aman, "His new studio means a lot to him, you know it is like,.......like a dream that is coming true, so much depends on this studio,.... it is his life's dream and of course, as he keeps saying that he will be ready for marriage once this studio comes alive,.......so,.......it is like a green signal for us to tie the knot now as he has established himself so well."

Sagar cannot believe what he is hearing, the world seems to close in on him, "What did you say?.....I mean, what was that thing about tying the knot?" Sagar asks Nita with a hope that she will tell him that he heard it wrong but alas, she breaks the sad news to him. "Aman and I will soon be married, we would have got married some months back but we took the decision to establish ourselves in our work before taking such an important step in our life," Nita tells Sagar who is getting choked and his ears are blocking all sounds from him as he is seeing his dreams getting shattered and there is no noise, no sound of his heart that has broken into a million pieces with Nita's statement. "Sagar, I don't know why but I really want to tell you that Aman and I are so much in love that we seem to be like two halves of the same soul. We have been together through the good and the not so good times alike, the togetherness through the times when things were not so smooth for both of us made our bond grow stronger as we helped each other walk out of our own shadows to a life we had sought out for," Nita says with her mind lost in Aman's thoughts. Sagar holds the table with a firm grip trying to face the pain that Nita has caused him, the shocking revelation of Aman and Nita's love, a tearing of his heart with an intense pain that makes him hate Nita and Aman for a moment moving into misery and regret for himself, an abruptly sad end to his saga of love, the pain is turning into tears that are moistening his eyes and choking his throat and he rushes out of Nita's cabin and out of Navigatory leaving Nita and Aman confused by his behaviour. "I cannot understand this man Aman, I don't even know why he was here and he just left without a word, strange, very strange," Nita tells Aman who is reading the newspaper at the office reception. "Don't worry he might have forgotten why he was here, let us leave for our new studio now," Aman tells her with a smile and Nita nods and they leave for the studio, another dream coming true in their life.

Sagar drives away in a frenzy collecting the remnants of his life that has been smashed to pieces in a bitter moment of truth, his dreams shattered and his love lost to another one, his pain is heart wrenching making him drive to nowhere for hours on the road before he realizes that he is still alive and left alone under the open blue skies, the brightness of the moon has faded with his sorrow and the world has cruelly deprived him his share of happiness, his love has been brutally strangled in the womb of his heart even before it could take birth and take its first breath. The love of his life is sadly unaware of the trauma he is undergoing, the pain he is living through, the misery his heart, mind and soul are smothered in as she is with Aman, the love of her life.

Chapter 26

Nita can see herself in Mona, the nervous little girl who had run away from an interview, the girl who got ridiculed and laughed at for fumbling, the nervous soul who created an imaginary world around her to support her, in fact, she created Mini to lend courage to her. She has become Mona's self appointed mentor and almost a Fairy Godmother to her. She has taken it as a challenge to make Mona a confident and strong person as a thanksgiving to the world for helping her gain her own confidence. Nita calls Mona to give her the first assignment at Navigatory. "Do you talk to yourself Mona?" Nita asks Mona. "No Ma'am," Mona replies nervously unable to understand the meaning and the purpose of her strange question. "Good, that makes things a little bit easier then," Nita tells Mona who is thoroughly confused at Nita's remark and wonders what prompted Nita to make this comment.

The first task assigned to Mona is to make a report on travel agencies in Saloni as Nita has to assess her real capabilities before she begins training her. Mona works on the report but is confused with the various terms used and the business parlance that are new to her. Mona tries her best to manage the report as she is fairly intelligent but her report is an average one leaving substantial room for improvement giving Nita an opportunity to pitch in to mentor and help her. Nita goes through the report in detail and knows she has to groom Mona to first improve her writing skills and then work on her presentation skills. Little does Mona know that she has been bestowed with such good luck that life has given her a mentor to help her through her life to make her walk out of her shadows to a world of brightness. Her life has definitely been designed with great favours from the Almighty. Nita asks her for a report every day and spends a lot of time in teaching her how to improve her writing skills and how to research for her reports. She goes through every detail as she plans to make Mona perfect in her skills so that she can create another manager for her business. It takes a week long effort to get a report from Mona that is up to the mark and Nita is happy that her training is yielding the desired results as things are gradually falling in place.

Nita asks Mona to make a presentation for her new clients that leaves her very nervous and she shudders in her fear of facing so many people. "I need you to make some slides and present them to me first," Nita tells Mona who keeps nodding though her heart is in her mouth from her nervousness. "So many people will be there, …….how will I face the people,……… what if I make a mistake or falter?" Mona thinks and gets more nervous. Mona sees Jugnu looking at her with anguish and knows she has to better herself and live up to Nita's expectations as she has been very patient with her and given her due time to improve so she knows she has to put in her best efforts in making the presentation. Mona takes a few hours to get the slides ready and informs Nita who asks her to make the presentation to her. "Your first presentation will be only for me, the next one for me and Jugnu and the third one for the clients. Let us see what you have here," Nita tells her as she looks at the presentation in detail with Mona standing anxiously waiting to hear Nita's comments. Nita is impressed with her slides and asks her to take her through the presentation in detail and she knows exactly what Mona must be going through. "Mona, just focus on the slides and forget that there is anyone else in the room and talk with your heart and soul. You need to do this well and we will keep repeating this till you perfect the art of presentation, so it is in your own interest to perfect it soon,…have your expressions in order as needed and pause at the right places for punctuations," Nita tells Mona who is looking at her with fear emerging and growing in her eyes. Nita smiles at her to encourage her and Mona starts to speak with feet trembling and her hands shivering from her nervousness. Nita knows she will need some more sessions of practice before she can face the clients and Nita has all the patience to groom her till she is satisfied with the progress that Mona is making with her skills and her confidence. She remembers how Mr. Kumar took them through the personality development classes to groom them and she is repeating all that she has learnt to help Mona come up the learning curve to the top of the charts. Life seems to have come to a full circle as she is moving through her past with Mona and reliving her story of success amidst failures and shortcomings with her as she moves through her struggles during her training period. She is confident that Mona will be able to manage though Jugnu thinks Nita is wasting her precious time on her and keeps grumbling to himself in his growing frustration. "Ma'am, I do not think you should spend so much time on Mona, we do not need to train people so thoroughly in the office, we expect them to get trained or self-train themselves on the job itself," Jugnu advises Nita. "I am aware of this fact Jugnu but I am different, I believe in creation and not in coronation. You will soon see her as an asset for our agency," Nita tells Jugnu. "Ma'am, what if she decides to get trained and leave us for our competition?" Jugnu asks Nita. "She won't, I am confident she will not leave us," Nita assures Jugnu who is still unsure about Mona. Mona feels obliged to learn and improve as she sees Nita spending so much time with her to bring her up the curve and this motivates her to better herself each time.

Nita meets Aman and tells him about her new venture of helping Mona discover herself, her crazy ideas of becoming a mentor for her, turning her office into a training ground where she is mentoring Mona. "That is commendable Nita. Your wanting to help someone is a very noble idea. It must make you feel so contented with life. Bringing a smile on someone's face is the greatest achievement that one can have and your efforts in helping the girl will be the highest attainment of your life, I feel so proud of you," Aman tells Nita with pride. Aman is glad that Nita is trying to help someone cross over the bridge of drawbacks and is delighted at the very thought of the incredible deed she has undertaken. Nita is thrilled to see the proud look on Aman's face which doubles her confidence and eagerness in helping Mona till the end till she sees the glow of confidence on her face. Three weeks later Mona is ready to present to the clients and Jugnu and Mona are with her when she makes her presentation about Navigatory and leaves them all impressed. They bag the contract with the new clients and Nita is the happiest person as she sees her efforts leading to fruitful results and she congratulates Mona on her success. "Mona, this success is not just about this contract, my joy is on your growth since you joined our business, the gradual turnaround of your personality and the new confidence that you have gained is what I am congratulating you for. You are now going to be an asset to our business and I am sure that you will help us get more and more contracts like these," Nita tells Mona who is thrilled on hearing Nita speak about her achievement. Mona is delighted and thanks Nita for the help, her patience and unrelenting efforts to make her gain confidence in herself. Nita just smiles and nods as she knows how Mona feels and is very happy for her and also with herself and she calls Aman to let him know about the day, the presentation and the confidence that Mona has achieved. Aman is impressed with Nita's dedication and helpful nature and knows that he has the best companion in the world.

Jugnu is not the only person who is feeling left out but Girish, another staff member from Navigatory gets envious as it is normal in a competitive world to see work colleagues vying with each other where rivalry builds up into negative energies and one sees the clones of Dani and Pam emerge creating issues at work impacting the growth of business. Girish sees a big rival in Mona who seems to be the favourite of Nita, the business owner and this starts reflecting in his rude behaviour towards Mona who is trying to bear with it as well as learning to put up to such rudeness which is in turn adding to her boldness as with every instance her confidence increases making her stronger.

Chapter 27

———✦———

Karuna is depressed at Sagar's shattered state and wants to help him but there is little one can do when a loved one has been unfortunate in love. She is staring at her grandson who has been unlucky in love, torn apart with the sense of rejection from the love of his life, a ruined soul drawn into the shadows of his grief which is overpowering him causing depression and a drift into loneliness, a life of recluse with the pain that is constant and severely devastating him.

Karuna knows she has to do something to help him before he drifts into a point of no return but the big question looming before her eyes is what should she do and how, she cannot speak to Nita as it will be of no use knowing that she is engaged to Aman and talking to Sagar will be futile as he is not in his senses but she still decides to talk to him. "Sagar, I can understand how you feel but life is not over yet,......life does not end with a failed attempt,....you cannot give up living as there are thousands of people whose life depends on you, your employees and your customers look up to you and you cannot grow weak in such a time,.....take a break, go for a holiday, away from Saloni for some days and come back as a new person who can take charge of his life,....we cannot let you waste your precious life. Things do not always move the way you would want them to,....we are helpless pawns who have to move with God's designs, ...He may have something else in store for you,....this could be a signal to let you know that you are chosen for some other path which He wants you to take, which life wants you to follow and change your life,....grief is a part of life but there is always a light at the end of the tunnel," Karuna tries to comfort Sagar who is lost in his own world. "I understand what you are saying grandma but life has turned for the worst for me, I feel so dejected and destroyed,....

life seems so meaningless,...I probably had too many expectations from life and it has suddenly slapped me and made me fall on my face,...why me? Why should I be the one who has to suffer? Why?" Sagar says as he is on the verge of breaking down. "Such are the designs of life, ...we have to keep moving on,...you could help others who are grieving, be with the ones who need help,...it might make you feel better, ...it is no consolation that there are others who are in conditions worse than ours but it is true and we cannot deny this fact of life,.......you need to work for the benefit of others now,..... it will help you carry your grief with you and things will slowly move ahead and you will learn to live with your sorrow, your problems,.......all I want to tell you is that I do not want you to ruin your life further,......you will have to take charge of yourself else you will go into a depression and ruin your health which will affect you, me and all those people who look up to you for their living,.......you need to walk out of darkness and face light and face life,.....get involved in your business,...open more hotels,....just get totally engrossed in your work so that your mind is so pre-occupied that it does not have the time to think about anything else, just drown yourself in work,...." Karuna tries to talk to Sagar who is trying to relate to what she has to say but is finding it difficult to come to terms with reality.

Sagar is lost in his grief and it is impossible for him to hear his grandmother's views and make an effort to understand her. He knows she means well for him and her wisdom comes from experience which is too vast and that makes him listen to her though with divided attention. He thinks through what she has said and speaks up after some time. "I will do as you say grandma, I will live for others,......I just need some time alone to face the truth of my life," Sagar tells his grandmother. "That is fine, if you make an effort things will surely start falling into place," Karuna tells him as she sees a ray of light that can help his grandson, he will have to learn to live with the truth of the designs of his life and move ahead for his people.

Chapter 28

Jagat Mansion has a new visitor, a young tall boy who is here to stay for some time with the Dutt family. Sunny alights from the train that has brought him to Saloni and takes a bus to Pawan Gardens to meet his uncle. He is wonderstruck seeing the expanse and beauty of the mansion and forgets the purpose of his visit to the city. He stands there for a long time till he is noticed by the guard who inquires about his whereabouts and sends him inside the bungalow to meet Jagat who has asked the guard to let Sunny in. Jagat is expecting him so there are no surprises from Sunny's visit and he is welcomed at Jagat Mansion by Sheela and Jagat and shown his room at the Mansion. Sunny, a tall and lean young man is a distant cousin of Aman who has moved to Saloni in search of a job though he does not intend to work for long. He is Jagat's younger brother Madan's son who has moved from Devon to Saloni with almost no ambition or aim as he has just been pushed by Madan to find a job and make a living in Saloni. Madan is a worried father, worried for Sunny's future as Sunny is what he calls 'good for nothing' and there are no efforts on part of Sunny to worry about himself and that adds to Madan's stress. This has forced Madan to send Sunny to Jagat, to the land of Saloni in a hope that he may wake up from his laziness and realize that he needs to make some efforts to sustain in this world. Madan has informed Jagat about Sunny's attitude and he wants Jagat to be strict with him. Jagat has taken charge of Sunny and relieved Madan from the duties, responsibilities and worries of fatherhood.

The mansion makes Sunny feel very regal and entices him to laze around in its comfort but Jagat knows he needs to be strict with him else he will not be able to fulfill his promise to his brother.

"Sunny, this is today's newspaper, just go through the job vacancies and start applying for jobs. I am giving you one week to find yourself a job else you go back to Devon," Jagat declares his harsh ultimatum to Sunny who is shocked to learn that he needs to find a job which he had planned to delay for some time as he wanted to spend some weeks as a guest at the mansion. Jagat knows he is being a little too harsh with Sunny but then he has to help him and this is the only way he can find to help. Sunny understands that he needs a job to make ends meet as he hears Jagat out and starts his job hunt and begins screening the job ads in the newspaper.

He meets Aman and they talk for a long time before day one for Sunny ends in Saloni. Aman suggests him to find placement agencies in yellow pages and call them up and his day two in Saloni starts with this activity but he does not meet with much luck. He starts meeting people from day three and knows he only has four more days before Jagat packs him off with his bags to Devon. His inherent interest lies in painting and he is impressed with Aman's works. He keeps leaving the confines of his room to meet Aman and watch him paint on his canvas in his room or on the terrace. Aman's paintings seem to tell him that he needs to take up painting as a profession but he knows his parents will not approve of his decision and the fear of their rejection discourages him to express his desire to them. "This is a beautiful painting," Sunny tells Aman when he sees him painting in his room. "Can I come with you to your studio tomorrow and see your paintings and learn to paint from you,.….will you teach me, Brother?" Sunny asks Aman. "Sure, you can, … but what about your job, did'nt you go for an interview this morning,.…what did they say?" Aman asks him. "Oh, ……….., I,……….I did not make it in time and they have finalized someone else for it," Sunny tells Aman sheepishly. Aman looks at him surprised and remembers his experiences with the various jobs he had managed to quit and smiles as he recalls those dark days of his life. Sunny expresses his desire to learn painting from Aman who agrees to help him on one condition. "Sunny, I will help you but you first need to find a job," Aman tells Sunny. This makes Sunny desperate to look for a job and he is ready to take up any job that he gets. Day six in Saloni, Sunny gets a job as a clerk in one of the hotels in Saloni and this gives him a pass to be at Aman's studio as a student. The hotel is close to Aman's studio which gives Sunny an hour at the studio before he goes to work, an hour with his passion before he gets drawn into the humdrum of the boredom of his job. Sunny makes a sketch the first day and Aman is not too impressed with it, a very average, rather below average sketch that is not up to any mark for Aman. He asks him to paint and finds that Sunny's strokes need a lot of improvement so Aman becomes his mentor to lead him through and teaches him the various nuances of his art. Sunny becomes a very regular student at the studio and makes every effort to learn which brings great satisfaction to Aman as a pupil's dedication is always appreciated by the teacher. Sunny's gradual improvement makes Aman proud as he sees that his efforts in teaching him have not gone in vain. He is reminded of Mr. Sharma every time he corrects Sunny or teaches him something new, a father figure holding a child's finger and helping him cross the road, the bridge from a land of learning to a land of perfection. His joy is unlimited and his pride beyond the boundaries of definition as the sapling he has been watering is growing into a large tree. The happiness that comes from making someone smile is divine and Aman is carrying the halo of this divinity with him! Sunny learns to paint like an artist as time progresses and helps Aman as an apprentice at his studio.

Aman wants to test his skills and asks him to paint something that defines his life and his struggle to explore the real artist within him. Sunny struggles for days as he paints and repaints on his canvas till the time he is convinced that he has perfected the painting. Aman is impressed seeing him spend long hours at the studio to make a masterpiece that would depict his innermost feelings. It is a moment of pride for Aman to judge his work, a painting of a fisherman trying to tether a boat to a pole amidst giant waves rising in wrath in an attempt to capsize the boat, a befitting depiction of his struggle and his efforts to support himself amidst all problems in his life. The colours and effects are so perfectly blended that Aman stands wonderstruck seeing the painting. Aman has tears in his eyes, tears of joy, of pride and jubilation for the work Sunny has created. Sunny is standing confused as Aman has not commented on his painting making him feel worried that his painting has not passed the test. Aman immediately calls Nita to his studio, "Nita I want you to come over to my studio as fast as you can, there is something that you have to see now." Then he calls his parents to join him at his studio adding to Sunny's nervousness making him fear the news that Aman is going to give to the family. Nita, Sheela and Jagat rush to Aman's studio in a state of panic assuming some untoward happening to have taken place at the studio but to their surprise Aman takes them to Sunny's painting in utmost pride and with a sense of achievement as he shows them his student's work which has brought him extreme fulfillment.

Nita cannot stop admiring the painting and congratulates Sunny on his beautiful and touching creation. Sheela and Jagat also appreciate his work and feel delighted to see the awesome painting. Jagat immediately calls Madan to congratulate him on his son's attainment and Aman tells Sunny he will sell this painting to an Art Gallery. "Sunny, this painting will fetch you handsome returns! You have become a true artist today and this is truly your masterpiece! I am sure you will make many more masterpieces and set up your own studio soon," Aman tells Sunny who is absolutely elated at hearing them all talk highly of his work and praising his creativity. Sunny cannot stop thanking Aman for his guidance and patience in training him to become an accomplished artist. Nita feels very proud of Aman and her pride and happiness glance at Aman through her tears as Aman gestures to her to stop crying and takes her for a stroll at the Maxing Garden which is Aman's favourite hideout since his childhood.

Chapter 29

Aman's favourite 'thinking bench' seems to be overjoyed sharing Aman and Nita's happiness. Aman is tasting the joy of helping Sunny find success, a joy that cannot be described in words but can be felt by the soul. "You must feel extremely satisfied today, it must be a glorifying moment to see your pupil excel in his art, Aman," Nita asks Aman who moves his fingers through her black tresses to clear them away from her cheeks. "Yes, it is a wonderful feeling, a victorious and ceremonial sensation that I am unable to explain to you," Aman tells a smiling Nita who is lost in Aman's eyes. Aman hears thunder and looks up at the skies that are covered in dark clouds and there are streaks of lightning moving across the sky announcing the arrival of rain. "It is about to rain, let me drop you home," Aman tells Nita reluctantly, finding it difficult to part from her. "Okay," Nita replies with reluctance too as she does not want to leave Aman and return home. But they walk to Aman's car and Aman drops her at Ashiana. "I will meet you tomorrow morning, need to discuss something with you," Aman tells Nita. "You can tell me now," Nita replies. "No, I need a reason to meet you tomorrow," Aman smiles at her. "Do you?" Nita says as she gets off the car. "I will meet you tomorrow," Aman bids her goodbye and leaves for Jagat Mansion.

Aman and Nita find it difficult to sleep missing each other, waiting for the sun to return with the morning and arrange for them to meet. Aman comes to Navigatory early morning to bring smiles and cheers in Nita's life. "You make my day with your smile," Aman says to Nita in his exhilaration. "And you make my day with your presence," Nita replies cheerfully. "So what was it that made us wait for the morning, what did you have in mind that you wanted to talk about or was it just an excuse to meet me this morning?" Nita teases Aman but Aman is lost in some thoughts. "No, I have

something serious and important to discuss with you Nita," Aman tells her.
"So please sit down and listen to me carefully as I want your views on my
suggestion as we need to take a decision about it," Aman tells an inquisitive
Nita who is curious to know what Aman has in mind.

"Nita, I have been thinking about Mona and Sunny. We have been
able to help two people but there are so many others we can surely help.
We found the help and support when we needed it and now it is time for
us to lend that support to others who need it more than we do. I have been
thinking of opening an academy for arts and personality classes where we
can teach others and help them come out of their shadows. We could take
the help of our friend Ravi and of Mona and Sunny to start the academy,"
Aman confides in Nita about his future plans astonishing Nita as she feels
he has read her mind. "Yes, of course, I have had similar thoughts several
times and wanted to discuss them with you. I am so glad that we always
think on similar lines. Let us open an academy called the.......'Manita'
Academy for Arts and Personality Development, ...Manita like Aman
and Nita said together very quickly, we could even call it Amanita, ...
no I think Manita sounds better," Nita suggests to Aman. "Wow, that is
a beautiful name,.....Manita,.....hmm, let us do it then and we can get
married on the day of the launch of the Academy,.......I mean if you agree,"
Aman asks Nita. Nita's joy knows no bounds, "Of course, we will get
married on the launch of the Academy. But why not before the launch?"
Nita asks Aman. "Oh,......we can,.....but if we take such a decision we will
work overtime to get Manita up and running in no time," Aman explains
to Nita who agrees with him. Their marriage seems to have become an
award and a reward for launching the Academy and is sufficient reason
to build their enthusiasm to work on the launch with great speed. "So
what are we waiting for, let us organize the launch, ...the land, funds,
building, faculty,.........and get married," Nita says cheerfully to Aman
who is thrilled to hear Nita speak with so much excitement and they start
planning the Academy as their marriage, their life and everything related
to their happiness depends on it, Manita seems to hold the key to their
happiness now.

They inform their parents of the decision to open Manita which is welcomed by them and Shan, Kaya, Jagat and Sheela are all very excited to learn about this new business which their children are going to venture into.

Ravi is thrilled at the thought and is eager to join them in this project. "I think it is a very noble thought and we should launch this Academy very soon. I am sure it will benefit thousands and millions of people over time. It sure is a great idea," Ravi tells Aman in an excited tone. Aman and Nita are happy to have Ravi by their side in this project as he is a man who knows how to get things done and has good contacts with builders and contractors. Aman knows Ravi is the only person who can be most helpful in this significant project that they plan to launch. Nita knows that Mona and Sunny have been groomed well by them and they have confidence in their abilities and capabilities to support Ravi in this project to realize their dream. Aman agrees with Nita's choice and knows the team of Ravi, Sunny and Mona will be able to translate their dream into reality.

Nita starts imagining the building of Manita and its layout which seems to keep her pre-occupied at all times as Manita is a dream of their life. Aman cannot hide his anxiety about Manita and that starts reflecting in his paintings too. Nita is surprised to see Aman make a sketch of a brown brick building with two smaller buildings on the side and sprawling lawns in front, the image of Manita in his mind. The sketch looks so beautiful that Nita cannot wait for Manita to come into existence. "Yes, this is how it should look like, I like the little silhouettes of students in the lawns and the building,….look there are some people peeping from the windows of the building,…reminds me of us looking out of our classroom windows,….I can almost see myself walking through Manita," Nita tells Aman excitedly. "It is my imagination of what Manita should look like and I will show it to Ravi, Sunny and Mona to let them know what I have in mind. I want Manita to be just like this, don't you, Nita?" Aman asks Nita. "Yes, this is just perfect and Manita has to be exactly like this," Nita agrees and takes a picture of the painting to share with Ravi on mail.

Chapter 30

Nita and Mona are at the Sagar Group of Hotels office to meet Sagar for signing the contract for his new hotel that has come up near Saloni. It worries Sagar to meet Nita as he is unsure of how he would react on meeting her, probably give himself away or break down but he decides to attend the meeting himself and not delegate to someone else in his office as he does not want to let Nita feel that he is undermining her efforts in providing travel services to his company. Sagar is also hesitant in meeting Nita as it hurts him to see her and not be able to let her know how he feels for her and he has to make dire efforts to suppress his feelings which are bursting from the seams of his heart but he has to meet her for business which is unavoidable. He stands there admiring her and her presence brings a fresh breath of happiness which is alas short lived as it soon dawns on him that she can never be his and that makes him miserable. Mona notices the look in Sagar's eyes and his expressions that speak of his immense love for Nita. The three of them discuss the contract and sign off on the agreement as Sagar looks at Nita with a lost look as he hurts himself each time he meets her.

Nita's mobile phone rings and she smiles seeing Aman's number and excuses herself out of the room to take his call. Mona can sense Sagar's feelings for Nita and she wants to talk to him but stops herself, thinks again and finally decides to speak to him. "Do you love her,.....do you love Nita Ma'am?" she surprises Sagar with her question. Sagar looks at Mona and is filled with distress and some respite as it is the first time that someone has questioned him about his love and at a moment when he really needs someone to talk to. "Yes, I do. But then what difference does it make,...... she loves Aman,.....life is too complicated, is it not? This is the bitter truth that is very painful," Sagar confides with such ease in Mona that it surprises him too. "I know how you feel,...have been through a similar state but then there is no option but to live with the truth and fight with yourself to survive,......there is nothing one can do,......but do you really love her or are you just infatuated with her personality? I know I am being rude but this is the question you need to ask yourself. Love will leave deeper wounds on your soul but infatuation is something you will easily get over with in no time at all. Lost love which is true love never heals itself. You just learn to live with its pain." Mona tells him with a straight look on her face as he listens to her keenly with his heart in pain and his mind finding a little comfort in talking to her and hear her speak. Her words seem to have an alleviating effect on him and he wants her to continue talking and lessen his pain. It is a strange statement that she has made, it brings a doubt in his mind whether he actually loves Nita or is infatuated with her and he wants to seek an answer to this question. "How do you differentiate the two, love and infatuation?" Sagar asks Mona. "Do you miss her each moment, even when she is with you? Do you see her in every little thing? Do you think about her happiness alone? Would you love her even if she had a different face? Would you be willing to die for her? Would you care for her even if she got married to someone else? Would you consider her happiness above yours? Would you decide to stay single all your life if you could not marry her? Do you feel her pain and sorrow as your own? Do you hear her thoughts even when she is quiet? Or do you like her for her beauty, her personality, her charm, her career? Have you felt the same way for other women who were doing well in their career or who were as charming as her?" Mona continues, "These questions will help you find the answer you seek." Sagar looks at Mona in admiration and is happy to have spoken to her. Mona has suddenly turned into a mentor and friend for Sagar who needs help at the moment to walk out of the darkness of his life. He smiles after weeks of living in sorrow and thanks Mona, "Thanks so much, I already feel better having spoken to you, it means a lot to me."

"Aman, I am at a meeting,.......I am at Sagar's office, ...I will be free in sometime,......will come to your studio immediately after leaving from here," Nita tells Aman who is missing her and wants to meet her soon. "Don't take too long, I must see you soon else I will destroy all my paintings, ...am

missing you too much, can't wait to see your beautiful dark brown eyes,.......
don't mess with your hair just let them stay on your cheeks," Aman tells Nita
who is smiling on hearing him talk like a small child. "I will be there as soon
as I can and please don't punish your paintings,......and I am not messing
with my hair, I am just moving them away from my cheeks," Nita giggles
as she talks to Aman who hears her giggles which seem to have a dreamy
effect on him. "Your voice makes me dreamy, I love to hear your giggles and
sense the smile on your pretty lips,.......I miss you more now, come soon,......
love you," Aman tells Nita who is smiling now, a smile that is turning into
a blush making her cheeks turn pink. "Yes, I will be there soon, let me just
say bye to him and move out from here,.......then drop Mona and come to
the studio,...okay,....bye,.......love you," Nita replies and puts her mobile in
her handbag with a smile on her pretty face that is illuminating her eyes
as she thinks about Aman and starts missing him too. Nita thinks about
Aman and shakes her head as he is clouding her thinking abilities again.
"I have to finish this meeting soon and go to the studio else........you never
know what Aman might do to his paintings, Aman you are again entering
my thoughts and,.......I need to finish this meeting and rush out soon,.....
don't know why Aman is behaving like this today, I have never seen him
get so restless before," Nita tells herself as she walks back to Sagar's cabin.

Nita comes back after attending Aman's call and looks at Sagar
apologetically, "Sorry, I had to take this call, it was urgent. Sagar, I think
we will take your leave now as the documentation has been completed.
Hope we will be able to service the new hotels well too. Mona will be in
charge of the new hotel business and your staff can get in touch with her
for any requirement. I am sure she will manage the contract very well."
Sagar nods as he looks at Mona adoringly and smiles, "Thanks Nita, I
am sure Mona will be able to manage the business well with her clarity of
thought and experience," Sagar replies bringing a smile on Mona's lips and
a confused look on Nita's face as she wonders how Sagar can talk with so
much confidence about Mona's abilities without having worked with her.

Nita and Mona get up to leave and Sagar sees them walk out of his cabin
and he can hear Mona's words echoing in his mind helping him clear the
haze from his thoughts and giving a new outlook to his life. He did have

similar feelings for other women in the past which had vanished with time and he had got over with his feelings easily. This too seemed like a similar instance and he can see himself coping easily with it. "Mona was right, I was infatuated by Nita's charm,….probably her charisma,…..her glowing and overflowing confidence,…..I do not think it is love,…..it is infatuation,…. yes, it is,…..it is just an infatuation for her,…..I feel the weight from my heart moving away making it feel so light." Sagar is smiling and is at peace with himself thinking about Mona and he seems to be impressed with her and probably infatuated with her too. "Life seems so simple after speaking to Mona, she helped me see through my life with such amazing ease that my pain has disappeared within minutes of talking to her." Sagar has been emancipated from his pain and feelings for Nita that had rendered him helpless and drowned him in sorrow making his life seem meaningless but Mona had brought a sudden enlightenment in his life which brought him back to himself like a person who has just woken up from a dream and has no reminiscence of it at all. He has Mona to thank for his liberation from the ambiguity of his life, a girl who may not have a beautiful face but has a beautiful soul who has brought back the smile on his gloomy face and peace in his life.

Nita steps into Aman's studio which seems relatively quiet making her wonder why she is not able to hear Aman or Sunny. "Aman,…..Aman,…. where are you?" Nita calls out to Aman but there is no reply which leaves her confused as Aman was forcing her to leave every work and come to his studio some time back and is nowhere to be seen now. There is a sudden flash of light and she is surprised to see herself covered in confetti and rose petals and she hears soft music in the background and there is a chorus of, "Happy Birthday to you…" from Aman, Kaya, Shan, Jagat, Sheela, Ravi, Sunny, Simi and Ajay who have been invited by Aman to celebrate Nita's birthday. Nita is amazed to see the beautifully decorated studio and the grand cake waiting for her in the centre of the studio hall. "I had completely forgotten that it is my birthday today………thanks, thank you so much,……," Nita is at a loss of words as she gets very touched with all their love. Kaya and Shan hug her and wish her. "But we could not have forgotten your birthday,…...and Aman wanted to have the party here,"

Kaya tells Nita who is almost in tears as her happiness is turning her too emotional. She looks at Aman and her eyes thank him as he stands there smiling looking at his lady love. Others congratulate Nita and ask her to cut the cake. "Thanks Aman, I am touched,.....this is why you were asking me to hurry up and reach your studio,....and I was wondering what was making you so pushy and why you were insisting repeatedly for me to leave all my work and head for your studio," Nita tells Aman with her twinkling eyes. Aman nods his head and smiles at her. Her happiness means the world to him and brings a feeling of extraordinary contentment that makes him feel so much at peace.

"We are all going out for dinner now," Aman announces and they leave for Nita's favourite hotel. Aman and Nita's parents get a chance to talk at length and know each other better. Nita and Aman overhear their mothers discussing their wedding arrangement which brings a smile on their faces and a relief that they have taken a liking to each other which means a lot to their relationship. Shan and Jagat also get along well which is very satisfying for Nita and Aman who value their families and want to see a strong bonding between their families for their married life to prosper. The dinner gives them all an opportunity to be together and share their bond and their happiness alike. "Aman, it was very thoughtful of you to invite our parents for this party," Nita tells Aman as she looks at their parents enjoying their meal. "You know I am very thoughtful and smart, I knew this would work,.......one dinner and your parents will be my fans for life,.......easy," Aman teases Nita who frowns at him and starts to giggle. "No, seriously speaking, I wanted us all to be together as this is our family now," Aman tells Nita who is looking at him with great admiration. "I am fortunate to have you in my life. You are always very thoughtful," Nita replies with great joy and fulfillment. The families are bonding well and Ravi, Simi and Ajay are also getting to know each other while Nita and Aman are in a different world altogether, a world where heavenly bliss is pouring in a shower on them, the chosen ones by life's own designs.

Chapter 31

Sunny is trying his hand on a new canvas when Aman calls him to speak to him about the Academy. "Have you ever thought of taking up a job for a living or are you going to while away your time here in the studio or at the hotel where you spend some hours every day," Aman asks Sunny who looks at him questioningly. "You need a job. Your paintings may not always sell for good sums so you need to create a backup plan to support you in life. You need to have a proper job where you work for a salary. You cannot just hang around here and there and be a rolling stone." Aman talks to Sunny in an assertive tone and feels he is talking like his father Jagat now and probably repeating the same words that his father had used for him in the past but he feels it is the right thing to say realizing that his father was right in questioning him and his concerns about him were very valid.

"Are you up for a job?" Aman asks him another question. "Yes, I am going to get a good job soon," Sunny replies with doubts written across his face as he is unsure of how and where to look for a job. "What kind of a job do you have in your mind? Have you met anyone or given any interviews lately?" Aman asks Sunny. "Something,……something that can give me independence to work and where I can make things happen, something where I can use my creativity, where I can create and build,…..probably," Sunny says as he thinks about what he would like to do. Sunny is surprised at discovering what he would really like to do. "Okay, then I have just the right job for you. I am going to give you a job where you will be earning well but you will need to earn it, you will have the independence to work and you will be given a lot of chances to make many things happen," Aman tells a surprised Sunny who is trying to guess what work is Aman talking about. Aman tells him about the Academy and how he would like it to be shaped up. "Sunny you will help in setting it up and you will also be responsible for the arts class at the academy. So, what do you think?" Aman asks him. Sunny cannot contain his excitement and jumps up at the proposition as this is like a dream come true, a dream walking out of a scrap book making things real for him. Aman is happy to see Sunny's excitement and knows that he has selected the right person for the job. "We are meeting here after two days to decide on the course of action and I want you here to attend the meeting, ...you will get a good salary for what you do and I want your complete dedication and hard work to get things rolling," Aman tells Sunny who keeps nodding his head in agreement with his mind taking him to a plot of land where he is visualizing the building and campus of the academy and sees himself teaching oil painting to his students. Sunny's joy is unlimited and his excitement is turning into a smile beaming till his ears as he cannot wait for the meeting to take place. Life has suddenly found its meaning for Sunny who is going to be a part of a very important project.

"By the way your new painting, the one with the backdrop of a village, will sell for a good twenty five thousand rupees," Aman tells Sunny. Sunny is delighted and unable to contain his happiness, "Twenty five thousand!! That must be a huge sum of money! I cannot imagine my painting is going to fetch such a big amount!" Sunny is amazed at the thought of earning so well from his painting. "I wanted to sell this one first so that you can get a better amount for your painting of the boat," Aman informs Sunny who is on seventh heaven. "Sure brother, you are the best judge," Sunny tells Aman. "You will soon have to start interacting with the galleries yourself Sunny. I will introduce you to them but I want you to be on your own soon,..... have a studio of your own,....be independent so that Madan Uncle gains confidence in you," Aman tells him as he thinks of setting up a separate studio for Sunny. "I will do as you say, I know you mean well for me, I am okay with whatever decision you take for me, your decisions are always the best," Sunny agrees with Aman's suggestions.

Chapter 32

Mona has to meet a new client and is working on her presentation, going through every slide in detail and memorizing the bullet points of her presentation unaware of the jealousy that is cropping up in Girish's mind. Girish is looking at Mona with extreme envy with his mind running in all directions trying to think of ways to ruin her presentation while Mona is busy with her work. Jugnu calls Mona with her presentation and they discuss it with Nita. Jugnu is trying to come to terms with Mona's presence in the office with a slow realization of her abilities that are not as dissatisfactory as he had assumed them to be. Mona and Nita discuss about their new client Pawan Singh who is very influential and rich with various offices spanning across Saloni and other cities implying a good opportunity for Navigatory to get good and recurring business. "Our presentation needs to be very effective if we need to crack this deal," Nita tells Mona and Jugnu. "I want to see the presentation before we leave for Pawan Singh's office," Nita tells Mona. Mona gets her laptop to Nita's cabin and is unable to power it leaving her shocked and torn and she desperately tries and retries and realizes that her laptop has crashed and she starts to cry profusely. "Mona,……listen to me,….Mona,……..stop crying and tell me if you have your presentation saved in some other computer or a pen drive," Nita asks Mona without getting disturbed at all. Mona looks at her confused trying to understand her as her tears have blocked her thought process. She thinks for a minute and remembers having saved it in a pen drive, a smile appears on her face and she runs out of Nita' cabin. Nita and Jugnu follow her to her seat where Girish is standing looking at Mona. Mona opens her cabinet and brings out a pen drive that has a copy of her presentation. "Here Ma'am, I have it here in this pen drive," Mona shows her the pen drive and notices Nita looking at Girish whose face had a cunning smile on seeing Mona running around which has disappeared on seeing the pen drive in her hand. Nita knows he is the culprit and looks at him sternly, "Girish, I want your help in getting Mona's laptop repaired since you know a lot about laptops and computers and I want it done before the day ends, else I want you to buy her a new one," Nita looks at Girish with fire in her eyes which is telling him that she knows he has done something to Mona's laptop and is announcing her judgement and his punishment in the same breath. Girish does not plead his innocence as he can sense it would be futile looking at the fuming anger in Nita's eyes. Nita, Jugnu and Mona return to Nita's cabin to finalize the presentation and Mona is thankful to Nita for believing in her and helping her out in this troubled situation. "These Pams, Danis and Girishs are stalking the good world around and they are like parasites who can never leave any opportunity to create problems for others," Nita mumbles to herself as Jugnu and Mona look at her trying to comprehend her statement. Mona is impressed how Nita kept her calmness and did not get perturbed knowing that Mona's laptop had crashed. Mona is fascinated with Nita and wants to walk tall like her and face life with total confidence and courage and she tries to listen to all her comments about the presentation with an aim to improve herself. Nita likes her presentation and they leave for Pawan Singh's office with a wish to get the deal from him while Girish is left frustrated as his efforts to ruin Mona's work have been in vain.

"I have another assignment for you Mona, a work that will be a little different from this one but I know you will manage it with ease and you have the expertise required for it," Nita tells Mona as they are driving towards Pawan Singh's office. Mona is delighted to hear her and is happy to know that she has been chosen for an assignment that seems like an important one. They are able to get the deal from Pawan Singh who has heard good feedback about Navigatory and has great confidence in their ability. Nita, Mona and Jugnu return very excited and perked up as they have a huge business to handle.

Nita calls Mona to explain to her about Manita and why she is choosing Mona for the new job. "It will be a new assignment altogether. You will help in setting up this Academy and also be in charge of the classes for

Personality Development. Do you think you find this job challenging? Are you willing to take it up? Of course, you will have other people to help you out with the setting up of the Academy. We have Ravi and Sunny who will be a part of the core team to manage the initial setup." Nita asks Mona who is gaping at her in astonishment as she cannot believe that she has been selected for such a coveted assignment. Mona is unable to respond as she is overjoyed and does not know how to react to this assignment which is going to be an enterprising challenge and she immediately agrees to be a part of the project. "I am so delighted that you found me capable of handling this project. I am surely going to be a part of it. I just cannot wait to take the classes and mentor others just like you mentored me. It is going to be an assignment of a lifetime with success with each student I will mentor. I am too excited and want to work on it immediately," Mona tells Nita with smiles all across her face. "Good, we are all meeting tomorrow at my fiance's studio to discuss this, I will let you know when to meet us," Nita tells Mona and is happy to know that Mona will be working with them as her dedication will go a long way in bringing the academy to life. Mona is lost in her thoughts of the new world that is waiting for her to move her to a different platform where she will be able to use her skills to build something new and also help others and this makes her feel joyous.

Chapter 33

Mona gets a call from Sagar for a meeting. Mona keeps all the invoices, receipts and files ready for Sagar Group of Hotels before she heads for its office to meet Sagar Rai. She is a little nervous as this is the first meeting she is going to meet a client alone. She has always had Nita by her side who could pitch in to answer difficult questions posed by the clients but she is all by herself today and that makes her a bit anxious. She scans the papers in her hand and prepares herself for the meeting by taking a deep breath before entering Sagar's office and walks in with her head held high. "I can do this with ease," she reassures herself and walks up to Sagar's cabin.

Sagar is elated to see Mona as he cannot wait to let her know how he feels. "Hi Mona. I have been thinking about our last meeting and since then your words have been haunting me,.......and you have been haunting me, you seem to keep appearing in my thoughts to make me restless, your words keep resounding in my memory," Sagar tells Mona who looks at him surprised as she expected the meeting to be about business and not personal issues. "I remember you asked me some questions and I have the answers for you.

Do you miss her each moment? Yes, I miss you every moment Mona, have been missing you each minute since we last met and even now when you are with me. Do you see her in every little thing? Yes, I see you everywhere Mona, everywhere and in everything. Do you think about her happiness alone? Yes, I think about your happiness, I can only think about your happiness now. Would you love her even if she had a different face? Yes, as I love your soul that is so beautiful, I would love you even if you had a different name or a different face Mona. Would you be willing to die for her? Yes, I can die for you, for your happiness, yes, I can Mona. Would you care for her even if she got married to someone else? I will not let you marry anyone else but if God is unkind and lets you marry someone else I will still care for you Mona. Would you consider her happiness above yours? Yes, all I can think of now is your happiness. I will do anything to see a smile on your face Mona. Would you decide to stay single all your life if you could not marry her? Yes, I will stay single all my life if I cannot marry you, I will actually kill myself if I am unable to marry you. Do you feel her pain and sorrow as your own? I will never let you be unhappy and I will feel your pain and sorrow as my own and above mine. Do you hear her thoughts even when she is quiet? I want to hear your thoughts and read your mind and I assure you I will soon be able to read your mind. I will. I like you for who you are and nothing else matters. I have never felt like this for any woman before. I am really in love with you. Will you marry me?"

Sagar has Mona speechless as he tells her how he feels for her and asks her for her hand in marriage in the same breath. Mona is confused by his long speech and puzzled at his sudden question and she can see genuineness in his disclosure of his love for her. She feels she must be dreaming and this cannot be real for sure. She is wondering what prompted him to like her as she is not pretty and not as charming as Nita or the other women he knows and this leaves her bewildered as she cannot reconcile to the fact that a man can love her for who she is and not what she looks like. It is a battle of the mind and the heart, 'Why would he love her?' is a question that Mona is unable to find an answer to. She knows life with an accomplished person like him would be very comfortable and she is a very realistic person who gives importance to the material life as she thinks money can buy everything and comfort can bring happiness. She is not sure whether she has any feelings for Sagar or not but she feels that a life of richness is of prime importance and love can follow later. She has seen a life of wants and needs as her parents are not well to do and she comes from a family of five children and a life of difficulties which makes her prioritize comfort and wealth above the rest. Sagar's proposal is definitely alluring and she is almost ready to agree and accept him. "You do not know what you mean to me Mona. You understand me so well that it leaves me amazed. You can hear my thoughts even when I am not speaking. I know for sure that it is not infatuation but true love that has touched my heart. I do love you." Sagar tells her as she looks at him judging him and assessing her own feelings for him. "It is better to marry someone who loves you rather than run after someone you love and who does not love you," Mona tells herself and nods. "Yes, I will marry you," Mona tells Sagar whose joy is limitless, a devotee whose prayers have been answered promptly. "I want you to meet my grandmother," Sagar tells Mona and they soon meet Karuna Rai whose happiness is overflowing with her tears of joy that she is unable to control on meeting her grandson's fiancee who has brought immense happiness in Sagar's life. Mona is happy to see her life taking a turn for the better on both personal and professional fronts that leaves her gratified and she thanks God for choosing her to shower his blessings on her.

Chapter 34

———◆———

Nita, Aman, Ravi, Mona and Sunny meet at Aman's studio the next day to discuss the plan for the academy, the land, contractors, buildings and resources. Aman declares he will fund the project as he looks at Nita with a twinkle in his eyes that comes to him naturally whenever he looks at her beautiful face and pretty dark brown eyes. Nita reciprocates his love with a smile and a cascade of love overflowing from the depth of her eyes as she looks at him with contentment as life seems beautiful when he is around her.

Nita tells them that the search is on for the land where the academy would be built but she has not been able to find a plot that can house such a big campus which they have in mind. Ravi comes to their rescue as always and calls his friend who is in real estate business and he suggests a plot of land near Ashiana which is available for sale. They leave to survey the plot that would determine the future of their life's dream and are impressed by its expanse and its location. The team of five looks around the plot and they all find it to be the apt location for the academy as it is within the city and easily approachable. "I think this is the best location, Nita," Aman tells Nita. Nita agrees and Ravi likes the plot too and approves of it instantly. The decision is taken and Aman decides to buy the plot immediately. The paper work is done within the next two days and construction work begins at the plot.

Ravi, Mona and Sunny shortlist the builders, contractors and other vendors who would bring the Academy to life. Ravi calls for quotations from various contractors and they try to find the most cost effective yet efficient contractors. Their lives have a new purpose and a new goal with the dream of the Academy turning into a reality soon. Mona and Sunny have never worked for such long hours till now but they are giving their two hundred percent to the project as it is a dream for them too. Life is making the five of them move ahead with the design of life falling in place making them take the right decisions and appoint the right people for every job in shaping the Academy. Manita is sure to come up soon as the devoted team is working hard and taking ownership of the smallest detail.

A week later it is a memorable day that is going to witness the commencement of the construction work at the site marked for Manita. Nita and Aman reach the site with their parents and Mona, Sunny and Ravi. They have organized for a 'bhoomipujan' before the work commences on the site as thanks to God for helping them buy the land and as a request to God for helping the construction take place smoothly. It is a moment of great joy and pride for the two families to see the dream of Manita coming alive. The land is cleared of all debris and the foundation stone is set for the work to begin with full gusto and Manita starts shaping up gradually. The site changes its layout and look within weeks as a mesh of scaffolding is visible all around it to allow for the building to come up gradually on the plot. Hundreds of labourers work through the day and night at the site and Manita begins to show signs of its birth as the ground floor becomes visible from a distance. Aman and Nita talk about Manita as though they are referring to a toddler who is growing into a small child and then a young man as this project is like their own baby.

"Nita, I think we should name our daughter, Manita," Aman tells Nita who is all smiles and beaming at the thought of having children. "Hmm,....yes,....Manita is a good choice, I think I like this name. We will surely call our daughter Manita,....and our son Nityam," Nita replies in a cheerful voice. "Nityam,...that is a nice name too,...Nityam,....NitaAman,.... Manita, Nityam," Aman replies and he keeps repeating the names Manita and Nityam in succession bringing a smile on Nita's face. They spend every evening strolling at Manita and oversee the progress at the site like watching a seed turn into a sapling and then a small plant and gradually a tree. Ravi joins them occasionally when he needs any approvals or suggestions leaving them alone for the rest of the times as he knows this is the only time they are getting to spend together after a long day at work. Walking through Manita is an extraordinary experience like walking through a dream that is shaping up, a divine consolation, a blissful joy from seeing the birth of a new life. Nita and Aman have found a new meaning in their lives with Manita.

Mona and Sunny are delighted to be a part of this grand project. Their dedication to the project is commendable as they put their heart and soul in finalizing each item to the minutest detail. They have emerged as successful winners in life changing their initial nature and attitude of laziness and nervousness to one of dedication and confidence. Aman and Nita appreciate the change in them and are happy to have selected them for this project. Those who learn to correct themselves grow into winners and overachieve in their enthusiasm to prove their worthiness. Sunny and Mona are two such individuals who are putting in their best efforts to outdo themselves to prove that they can manage any responsibility assigned to them. Their growth over past months is commendable and praises and appreciation from Nita, Aman and their parents is adding to their success. Ravi is a person of strong will and determination, a person who will extend every possible help to his friends and Manita is giving him every opportunity to prove his friendship. Nita and Aman feel blessed to have his support and cannot stop thanking him.

"Mona, it is really good to have you on this project. You and Sunny are gradually bringing Manita to life," Nita tells Mona cheerfully acknowledging her hard work. "Manita has been a project that needed a lot of patience and coordination to get things done in time, you and Sunny have really put your heart and soul in getting Manita into shape. I was apprehensive initially thinking that it may take a long time but you managed it well, I am very impressed at the speed of things and the selection of contractors who are equally devoted to our project," Nita tells Mona. Mona thanks her and informs her about her decision to marry Sagar which comes as a surprise to Nita. "Wow, are you sure of your love for him,…..don't get me wrong but I did not get to know that the two of you were in love," Nita asks Mona.

"I know what you mean. I am still not sure about my feelings. Sagar loves me. I know he does. I want to get settled in life and I just agreed when he proposed to me. I know I will have a comfortable life with him and I too will start loving him with the passage of time. It is good to marry someone who loves you and that is what I am doing," Mona tells Nita. "I asked because I wanted to be sure that you are aware of what you are doing and not just getting carried away in the moment. Don't get me wrong but I do find Sagar to be a little different,......I mean it is difficult to judge him as his actions get ambiguous at times but I am sure you would have good reason to take this decision. I just want you to be happy. I am happy for you in your happiness, all the best and wish that you both have a long and prosperous married life," Nita wishes Mona and hugs her as she is happy for her. "I know what you mean, I have met him a couple of times and am getting to know him. Settling down is important for me at this time as I come from a mediocre family and my parents will be happy to have one of their daughters married off. I cannot wait for things to happen for me on the marriage front as I am neither pretty nor rich and this proposal from Sagar is like a blessing from heaven as it is a match that was impossible for me to find myself. I know I will at least have a comfortable life with him and will eventually fall in love with him too," Mona tries to put Nita's worries at ease.

Nita is happy to see Mona's life take a beautiful turn and she wants Manita to be launched soon to marry Aman and get settled in her life. Aman's thought brings a heavenly smile on her face leaving her spellbound as she drifts into another world, a world where she and Aman will have a life filled with all happiness and they will walk through life together. She comes back to the room after a little while and asks Mona, "Mona, I hope you will continue with this project after your marriage too." "Of course Ma'am, I will. In fact I have spoken to Sagar about it and he knows that I will be working with you on this project. This project means a lot to me and I will continue to be associated with it," Mona tells Nita who feels relieved to hear that Mona will not move out of the project after her marriage with Sagar.

Chapter 35

An year later Manita is born to fulfill Aman and Nita's dreams and to fulfill the dreams of millions of students who will be flocking this academy to learn various arts and crafts and develop their personalities and emerge as winners in life. Manita stands tall as Aman and Nita behold it as their lifelong dream, a temple that would help its worshippers walk out of the shadows of their life, their drawbacks and failures limiting their success. It is a moment of pride and immense satisfaction when Nita and Aman enter the gates of Manita and take a tour of the campus with their friends Ravi, Simi and Ajay. The signboard of the academy 'Manita Academy for Arts and Personality Development' is put up outside the gate of the academy as onlookers stand as though they are witnessing a flag hoisting ceremony. Mona and Sunny feel honoured when they are given the roles of teachers for the Personality Development and Art Classes. Their hard work has met with success and their new jobs are like awards for them and a challenge to mould and guide their students towards success. It is a moment of honour and of responsibility as they have to live up to the expectations set by Nita and Aman to be a guiding force and mentor for the students of the Academy. Nita and Aman request Ravi to take on the role of the Principal of the Academy and he accepts it with great pleasure and pride. The first session sees students flocking in to take admission in the various classes as they too want to succeed like Aman and Nita.

"It really is very satisfying to help someone, a feeling of great happiness from making another fight through their weaknesses, their drawbacks and shortfalls to achieve their dreams," Nita tells Aman with a sense of achievement. "Yes, Nita, you are right, real happiness comes from making someone else smile," Aman says in agreement. Nita and Aman feel the extreme sense of accomplishment from having helped Mona and Sunny, holding their hands and making them cross the bridge from a life of insecurity to a world of achievements and success. "This is the real success for us Nita," Aman tells Nita who smiles in her acknowledgement knowing that they have given a new definition to success today. Nita and Aman are walking in the lawns of Manita and sharing their happiness and remembering the time spent at the Arts School and its classes that brought them together and bonded them for life. There is immense pride in their eyes as they watch the brown brick building of Manita, a vivid translation of their dreams into reality where many dreams will be fulfilled in times to come as it will nurture the aspirations of the students who will walk into this building with great expectations and dreams of their future. Real happiness is not derived from coming out of your own shadow but by helping others move out of their shadows to achieve success in their life, the sunshine that makes you glow when you are standing with someone as a mentor brings out the joy from within that no money in this world can buy and Manita will be bringing this successful joy in many lives. They admire the students walking through the corridors and settling in their classes. Aman spots a young boy with an easel near the lawn and runs towards him in intrigue. The boy is painting some clouds on his canvas. Aman takes a brush and perfects the lines of the clouds as the boy looks at him in total admiration and says, "Wow!!" Sunny comes out from his class where he is helping another student and watches Aman paint. "Brother, we may all try hard but can never be as good as you are," Sunny tells Aman who just shakes his head. "No, it is not true, I am still learning," Aman says to Sunny and smiles at Nita as they start walking towards the main gate.

"Nita, do you want to go to the Maxing Garden?" Aman asks Nita. "Sure, why not?" Nita responds as she looks into his eyes to see her beautiful world. "But…why Maxing Garden?" Nita asks him. "Just want to visit my favourite thinking spot and let my bench know about Manita. Want to tell the trees that I am getting married to you. And tell them about Manita," Aman says as Nita listens to him with great interest lost in his eyes and his love. "Tell your bench and the trees!" Nita questions him in a naughty teasing tone. "Yes, tell my bench and my trees and my mountains, my valley, my skies and my moon, my stars and my sun. I have always told them about my worries and failures, it is rare for me to go and talk about my success with them, it is time I let them know about my happiness and my success too," Aman replies with Nita staring at him in awe. "Sure, let us go and break the good news to them too," Nita says as she runs in her excitement towards his car.

Maxing Garden is as beautiful as ever and Aman's favourite bench is vacant, ...perhaps waiting for Aman. "It is so peaceful here, Aman," Nita says as she looks around the garden and can see its beauty and calmness that makes Aman spend hours at this spot. "You are right, this place definitely has a life, a soul," Nita tells him. "These skies, the trees, the mountains and the valley have all been there with me during the ups and downs of my life and have seen me walk through every failure and manage it and I have spent several nights in the moonshine gazing at the stars. This bench had become an integral part of my life. I wanted to be here to let all my friends of nature know that I am getting married," Aman tells Nita as he looks around the garden which has a celestial bliss almost like a blessing for the bride and groom to be. Aman stands on his bench and declares his love to the world. "I love Nita and am marrying her tomorrow," Aman shouts at the top of his voice and the echoes of his voice are heard across the valley. Nita follows him to stand on the bench with him and cups her hands on her mouth to shout, "I love Aman and am marrying him tomorrow." Her echoes resound in the valley and entwine with Aman's echoes as an invitation to the world to attend their wedding. They both shout again together and their voices reverberate like a clapping of the skies, congratulating them on their wedding. The stars are unusually bright today with a blessing for Nita and Aman in their blissful shine that adores them and takes pride in their true success!

Chapter 36

The next morning is a day of extra brightness as the skies announce their happiness for Nita and Aman who are getting married in the lawns of the Manita Campus. The world is unusually cheerful and the sun has risen early to congratulate the couple to be. The breeze is making the chimes swing into songs of joy and the birds are chirping wedding songs for Nita and Aman. The skies are beautiful and clear and the heavens are showering their innumerable blessings and infinite love on Nita and Aman. Life is moving as per its best design as Nita and Aman have chosen the brightest colours of their soul to follow through its path and illuminate many other lives with its light.

Ashiana and Jagat Mansion are in a state of total pandemonium with guests in every corner of the house and hosts running around in all directions trying to confirm if all arrangements are in order and shouting last minute instructions to the servants. Ravi is overseeing the arrangements to ensure that the wedding of his best friends is just perfect and memorable. It is a special day for two special souls and their families and friends who are gathering to grace the occasion. The two homes are happiness personified with Aman and Nita dressed in elegant regal attires for their grand wedding, a handsome couple made for each other, their love has found a true meaning and life giving further strength to their bond of a lifetime. Nita looks like a princess in an elegant maroon attire and Aman, her Prince Charming is dressed in majestic golden beige.

Kaya, Shan, Sheela and Jagat are the proudest parents at the wedding, standing tall and joyous, their abundant joy compliments the beautiful flowers adorning the lawns and the soothing instrumental music playing at the venue. Ravi, Simi and Ajay are standing beside their two good friends to wish them at the special day of their wedding. There is a beautiful rainbow in the skies splashing its lovely colours across the world with wishes for the newlyweds whose life has become a rainbow for millions who will soon be guided and mentored by them. It is a wedding to remember with grandeur, true happiness and genuine smiles across faces and abundant blessings from every heart and soul. Mona and Sunny are the organizers of the big event having paid personal attention to every little detail and arrangement that will bond Nita and Aman into a happily ever after relationship of a lifetime with sunshine forever without any shadows!!

Nita and Aman hold their hands as they move into a new light leading the way for millions to follow!!

About the Author

Ranjana Kamo has a passion for writing. She wrote her first poem at the age of six. She has several publications to her credit. She likes writing about life and thought provoking subjects. She derives her inspiration for writing from real life experiences and observations of human behaviour. She is blessed with a close knit and caring family with whom she likes spending whatever time she can get.

She is a banker, a quality professional by choice with a Master Black Belt in Six Sigma. She has done her Chartered Accountancy, an MBA in Finance and BSc Mathematics Honours from the Delhi University.

Other titles by the author include –

1) "God Walks My Dreams", a modern day fiction and
2) "Treasured Forever", a collection of poems.